5/19

P9-DJL-320

I LOVE YOU,
MICHAEL
COLLINS

LAUREN BARATZ-LOGSTED

I LOVE YOU, MICHAEL COLLINS

East Bridgewater Public Library
32 Union Street
East Bridgewater, MA 02333
(508) 378-1616
www.eastbridgewaterlibrary.org

Margaret Ferguson Books

FARRAR STRAUS GIROUX

New York

This book is a work of fiction. It was not authorized, approved, licensed, or endorsed by Michael Collins.

Farrar Straus Giroux Books for Young Readers
An imprint of Macmillan Publishing Group, LLC
175 Fifth Avenue, New York, NY 10010

Text copyright © 2017 by Lauren Baratz-Logsted
All rights reserved
Printed in the United States of America by LSC Communications, Harrisonburg, Virginia
Designed by Andrew Arnold
First edition, 2017
5   7   9   10   8   6   4

mackids.com

Library of Congress Cataloging-in-Publication Data

Names: Baratz-Logsted, Lauren, author.
Title: I love you, Michael Collins / Lauren Baratz-Logsted.
Description: First edition. | New York : Margaret Ferguson Books / Farrar
   Straus Giroux, 2017. | Summary: In 1969, as her own family is falling
   apart, ten-year-old Mamie finds comfort in conducting a one-sided
   correspondence with the least famous astronaut heading toward the moon on
   Apollo 11. | Includes bibliographical references.
Identifiers: LCCN 2016038109 (print) | LCCN 2017008448 (ebook) | ISBN
   9780374303853 (hardcover) | ISBN 9780374303877 (Ebook)
Subjects: LCSH: Project Apollo (U.S.)—Juvenile fiction. | Apollo 11
   (Spacecraft)—Juvenile fiction. | Collins, Michael, 1930—Juvenile
   fiction. | CYAC: Project Apollo (U.S.)—Fiction. | Apollo 11
   (Spacecraft)—Fiction. | Collins, Michael, 1930—Fiction. | Space flight
   to the moon—Fiction. | Family problems—Fiction. | Letters—Fiction.
Classification: LCC PZ7.B22966 Iak 2017 (print) | LCC PZ7.B22966 (ebook) |
   DDC [Fic]—dc23
LC record available at https://lccn.loc.gov/2016038109

Our books may be purchased in bulk for promotional, educational,
or business use. Please contact your local bookseller or the Macmillan
Corporate and Premium Sales Department at (800) 221-7945 ext. 5442
or by e-mail at MacmillanSpecialMarkets@macmillan.com.

For Seth Baratz, older brother and first friend.
When we were little, you made me see things I never
would've seen on my own. You still do.

I believe this nation should commit itself to achieving the goal, before this decade is out, of landing a man on the moon and returning him safely to the earth.

—*John F. Kennedy, in an address
to Congress, May 25, 1961*

I LOVE YOU,
MICHAEL
COLLINS

Dear Michael Collins,

You're going to the moon!

Well, technically, you're not going *to* the moon. You're going *around* the moon. Neil Armstrong and Buzz Aldrin are going *to* the moon. But still . . .

You're going around the moon! It's very exciting!!!

Sincerely yours,
Mamie Anderson

Dear Michael Collins,

It's okay that you didn't write me back. I thought you might, even though I didn't ask specifically, because that is what people usually do when you write them a letter: they write you back. But maybe you were wondering, *Why is this kid even writing to me in the first place?* It's okay if you are. People wonder about me a lot. I think that's just something that happens when a person is not like other people.

Let me explain.

So there I was in class last week. It was the day before the last day before summer vacation. Our teacher, Mrs. Collins—

Don't you think it's funny that my teacher and you have the same last name? I do. It's like she's your wife or something. Which I know isn't true. You have an entirely different wife. I know, because I asked my teacher. And you're not Mrs. Collins's brother or brother-in-law or cousin either. I know, because I asked those questions, too. Still, it's kind of funny, right?

The questions about the names came later, but first what happened was this: Mrs. Collins asked us what we wanted to be when we grow up.

All the boys said they wanted to be astronauts. Billy Parker said it first. He didn't even raise his hand before answering. Then the other boys shouted the same thing.

"Girls?" Mrs. Collins said. "What about you?"

Delores Doyle's eyes got shiny, like Reverend Potter's do in church when he talks about God or like my mom's do when she talks about chocolate cake, and then she said, "I want to *marry* an astronaut!"

And you know something? She probably will. Delores Doyle's skirts are always the right length, she has perfect knife-straight hair, and she even has the deluxe set of Magic Markers, the one with every color in the world. Her dad got it for her in the city, which is where his job is. I asked my dad once if he could switch his job to one in the city, like Mr. Doyle's job, but he said that probably wasn't a good idea, not even to get Magic Markers. He said he doubted Mr. Doyle's law firm was looking to hire telephone linemen.

After Delores Doyle said she wanted to marry an astronaut, the other girls said the same thing.

Do you think that's strange? All the boys want to be

a thing and all the girls want to marry that thing? I think that's strange.

"What about you, Mamie?" Mrs. Collins asked. "Do you want to be an astronaut or marry an astronaut?"

I had no choice but to answer. Usually, I do my best not to answer things in class, because of the risks. But when your name is right in the question like that, it's unavoidable.

"Neither," I said.

"Neither?" Mrs. Collins said.

Was there an echo in the room?

"Then what do you want to be when you grow up?" Mrs. Collins asked.

"How should I know?" I said, throwing my hands in the air. "I'm ten!"

Some of my classmates started to laugh.

I tried to explain. "How should I know what I'm going to want to be so many years from now? Wouldn't it be foolish of me to try to predict—"

But apparently I was the fool, because my words were drowned out by more laughter.

See? That there. That's the risk. You open your mouth, and people laugh at you.

This time, though, it wasn't too bad, because Mrs.

Collins immediately shifted the class into the assignment part, which I guess was where she'd been moving all along.

"Today we're going to do something a little different," Mrs. Collins said. "Everyone knows that, in the middle of July, three astronauts are leaving from Cape Kennedy in Florida and flying to the moon. Can you tell me what their names are?"

People started shouting. If you ask me, Mrs. Collins has trouble controlling a room. Does your Mrs. Collins have that kind of trouble, too?

"Neil Armstrong!" people shouted.

"Buzz Aldrin!" people shouted.

"And Michael Collins," Mrs. Collins said when no one shouted anything else.

"And they're going on Apollo 11!" Billy Parker shouted.

"Very good, Billy," Mrs. Collins said. Then she wrote the three names on the blackboard: *Neil Armstrong, Edwin "Buzz" Aldrin Jr., Michael Collins*.

"The assignment," Mrs. Collins said, "is that I want you each to select one astronaut to write a letter to. I'll give you the address where you can send your letter, care of NASA. Okay, who wants to write to Neil Armstrong?"

A ton of hands shot up. But when the boys who put

their hands up noticed that nearly all the girls had picked Neil Armstrong, too, those boys immediately pulled theirs down. Mrs. Collins counted raised hands and then placed that many check marks next to Neil Armstrong's name.

"Why Neil Armstrong?" Mrs. Collins asked.

"Because he's so dreamy," Delores Doyle said.

"I can't argue with you there," Mrs. Collins said, laughing.

"And he's the commander," said Lisa Burke, who is Delores Doyle's best friend.

So apparently, in addition to wanting to marry the thing that the boys all want to actually be, the girls also want that thing to be good-looking and have lots of power.

"Okay, who's writing to Buzz Aldrin?" asked Mrs. Collins.

This time, every single boy in the room raised a hand. Some even raised both hands.

"He's got the greatest name!" Billy Parker yelled before Mrs. Collins could ask the question we knew was coming. *"Buzz!"*

"Indeed he does." Mrs. Collins laughed again. Then she counted hands and made check marks next to Buzz

Aldrin's name, just making a single one for each kid, even those who had both hands up. Once she was done doing that, she added up the total number of check marks. And once she was done with that, she turned around to the classroom, puzzled.

"Someone didn't select an astronaut to write to," Mrs. Collins said. Her gaze zeroed in on me. "Mamie? Did you pick an astronaut?"

There it was again: my name included in a question.

"Michael Collins," I whispered.

"I'm sorry," Mrs. Collins said, placing a hand behind one ear. "I didn't hear you."

"MICHAEL COLLINS!" I said.

I couldn't help it. There were those two other astronauts, with every check mark in the world beside their names. And there you were, with none.

"Oh." Mrs. Collins looked surprised. But at least she put a check mark beside your name, even if it looked kind of lonely up there by itself. "Can you tell us why?"

I couldn't. I couldn't say it was because when I saw all those check marks for Neil Armstrong and Buzz Aldrin but none after your name, it made me feel a weird kind of sad for you. So instead I said: "Because he's the best one."

That's when it really happened, so much worse than before. Everyone laughed at me. Even Mrs. Collins cracked a smile before covering her mouth with her chalky hand. The laughter, it was so loud, like in the *Peanuts* comic strip when Charlie Brown says something and the response to that looks like HA! HA! HA! HA! HA!, with HA!s as far as the strip allows, everyone laughing so loud it's like a tidal wave of sound that could knock a person over, just washing her out to sea.

"That's so stupid!" Billy Parker guffawed. "Michael Collins? He's not even going to the moon!"

"Of course he is," I said. Now who was the one being stupid? Everyone in the country except for babies and people in comas knew that three astronauts were going to the moon and what those astronauts' names were.

"Not really." Billy Parker had trouble talking, he was laughing at me so hard.

"What do you mean?" I said—and while I hate to use the word, it's the only one that applies here—dumbly.

Billy Parker took a deep breath and said with a bit more patience than I was used to from him, "Neil Armstrong and Buzz Aldrin are the ones who will walk on the moon. Michael Collins is just going to be orbiting it.

So he won't walk on the moon, not ever. He has to stay with the ship."

The whole class nodded. Apparently, this was common knowledge. But I hadn't known. I guess that's because I've kind of had a lot on my mind lately.

I thought of you then. I thought of you coming so close to the moon, how you'll be coming closer to it than all but two other people in the entire history of the world so far, and still you won't be able to touch it, at least not on this trip.

"Well," I said, folding my arms across my chest to show I meant business, "I don't care. I'm still going to write to him. He's still the best one."

Of course the laughter came again then, like a bucket of icy rainwater pouring over my head.

But that was okay, too, because this was the last assignment of the year and once we were done with our letters we started talking about Vietnam, which Mrs. Collins has us do a lot. I know it's an important subject, Vietnam, but sometimes it is hard to truly understand what is going on there since that country is so far away, particularly when a person is still in elementary school.

So now you know, Michael Collins. You know why I

wrote that last letter to you: because I had to. It was a school assignment, I said I'd do it, and I did it.

But this time? I wrote to you because I wanted to. I wanted to explain, and now I have.

Sincerely yours,
Mamie

Dear Michael Collins,

It's okay that you didn't write me back again. You're probably busy doing stuff to get ready for your trip. I know that whenever we go on a trip my mom draws up a list of everything we will need. She uses a legal pad and a separate sheet of paper for each family member. Just between us, I think it's a lot of extra work for nothing. We all need some of the same things, like socks and underwear, so why write it down more than once? Does she think if it's not on a list, we'll forget those things? Believe me, I've been told about the importance of clean underwear more than once, how it has to be that way in case an ambulance ever comes for you because you do not want to suffer the embarrassment of dirty underwear in such a situation—I'm not likely to forget about that!

And then there are the things that just one of us needs, like my dad and his shaving kit. Does my mom think that he'll only remember if he sees the words "shaving kit" on his list? Or does she think that if I don't have a list, I'll somehow pack a shaving kit for myself by mistake? That's ridiculous. I'm a girl!

But maybe, now that I think about it, the things you'll need for your trip are a little different from the things my family needs when we go to Lake George for our summer vacation, which is only every other year—my dad doesn't take much time off from work for any reason. Plus, I guess if you and the other astronauts forget something, and you realize it five minutes after leaving, it's not exactly like you can turn around and go back for it the way we always do.

Anyway, you probably want to know more about me and my family.

My parents are old. I'm talking about super old, Michael Collins, even older than you, I bet. No one in my grade has parents as old as I do, except for Delores Doyle, whose father is sixty. But her mom is only thirty, and my mom says that's a crime and not something we should ever talk about.

My dad is forty-four and my mom is forty-three. Do you see what I mean? Between the two of them, they are eighty-seven—that's almost ninety.

I already told you my dad is a lineman for the telephone company. He is tall and what you would call lanky. His hair is brown, and even though it looks just fine on him and my mom says he is still as handsome as when she first met him, it is not any of the special kinds of brown, and that's what I wound up with, too. People always say I take after my dad, and while his face looks fine on a forty-four-year-old man, I think it may take me some years to grow into it. As for my mom, she's a home-maker. She is also very particular about her appearance. Her blond hair is always perfect. She won't leave the house to throw out the trash unless she's got her pearls on, even when it's summer and she's wearing her Bermuda shorts.

Sometimes my parents fight about things. They say these are just "discussions," but I've had plenty of discussions with my best friend, Buster, and none of them ever sounds like that. My parents have always been like this, but lately it's getting worse and worse. Lying in my bed at night, listening to them have discussion after discussion, which mostly I can just hear the volume of but not the specific words, well, it is the opposite of fun.

My oldest sister is Eleanor. She is twenty-four and favors our mom in appearance and prettiness. Eleanor moved out of the house six months ago, which became another occasion for a "discussion." My dad said Eleanor shouldn't leave home until she's married. My mom yelled back that she didn't want Eleanor to get stuck leading the life she herself has led. My dad asked what was so bad about my mom's life. My mom said, "What life?" That part didn't make me feel so good. She also said she wished she'd waited longer to start a family. Somewhere in the yelling, Eleanor just quietly left. Now she has her own apartment.

My other sister, Bess, is sixteen. Bess looks like a cross between both our parents, and somehow on her it looks good, because she got the best of each. She has a boyfriend. That's pretty much all you need to know about Bess right now, other than that she's mostly okay. Well, except when she says stuff like "I was upset when I first learned Mom was going to have another baby. I didn't want the competition, but then it turned out to be you, which was no competition at all." Also, Bess is a hippie, which is not necessarily something my dad appreciates about her. Bess has long hair that is between blond and brown, and she likes to wear scarves tied around her head like a pirate, which I don't think does anything for keeping her cool in the summer like a ponytail would, but I guess that is not the point. She's not big on footwear these days, but anything with suede fringe attached to it, Bess will take it.

Eleanor, Bess, and Mamie.

Do you see what our parents did? They named each of their daughters after whichever First Lady happened to be in the White House on the day that daughter was born. Eleanor made it under the wire just before Franklin D. Roosevelt died in office; otherwise, we might have had two members of the family named Bess. Bess was born on New Year's Day, 1953, so she got the Truman vote. And I'm of course named for Mamie Eisenhower. That's bad luck for me. Just two years later, I could have been a Jacqueline or even a Jackie. (I think maybe a lot can be determined by a person's name. Who knows? Maybe if you were named Buzz, you'd be walking on the moon, too. Because I checked in the phone book and I hope you won't be offended, but let me tell you, even around here, there is more than one Michael Collins.)

So now you know about my parents and Eleanor and Bess.

And, of course, you already know all about me.

Sincerely yours,
Mamie

Dear Michael Collins,

There is one other important person in my life you should know about. Buster Whitaker is my next-door neighbor and best friend all rolled into one, has been since his family moved in there when we were both five—so, half our lives. The movers had barely unpacked their sofa when Buster yelled over, "Hey! You wanna play?" and I yelled back, "Okay!" And that, as they say, was that. Nobody, including me, knows what Buster's real name is. Well, obviously his family does. But outside of them? Buster says it is so awful, if people heard it they would just laugh and laugh. I don't think he realizes, but I would never laugh at Buster, because he is the finest person I know.

Also, what name could be so awful that "Buster" is an improvement on it?

One thing's for certain. It is a crime against the universe that Buster and I have never been in the same class. This means that during the school year, we have never been together outside of lunch and recess, so he wasn't in Mrs. Collins's class this past year, which is a shame because I know he would never have laughed at me when I said you were the best one. The good news is that now that it's summer vacation, Buster and I are able to be together from the time we get up in the morning until dinnertime and sometimes even beyond.

I will give you an example of what a summer day with Buster is like.

Today I get up at seven, brush my teeth, get dressed in orange shorts and a matching top, and go downstairs for breakfast, which is Cap'n Crunch. I do not care for Cap'n Crunch as much as some other cereals, but my mom says it is better for me than Froot Loops, which is my favorite. Froot Loops are just so much more colorful, and then after they soak in the milk for a bit, it is like having a bowlful of rainbow. Plus lots of sugar.

"Can I go over Buster's?" I ask my mom just as soon as the bowl is empty. My dad has already left for work.

"I don't see why not," Mom says, "so long as you two don't spend the entire day cooped up indoors."

I have learned that being "cooped up indoors" is something that adults are fiercely against kids doing, even though it is something adults do all the time. For example, after school in the winter, we have to put on our snowsuits and go outside to play, no matter how cold it is. This is the case even when we build an igloo and the snow somehow gets between our snow pants and our boots and then trickles down into our socks so our toes freeze and our feet feel like blocks of ice. We have to play outside until it gets dark. The cocoa afterward is good, but sometimes I think it is hardly worth the price of ice-block feet.

Fall and spring aren't too bad, but really, summer is no better than winter. You just can't escape the heat. By late morning, even the shade doesn't help much. And at night, it is so hard to sleep. In my house, we have two ways to get cool air. There's a portable fan that gets moved from room to room depending on who's doing what. So if my mom is cooking, it's going to be in the kitchen, and when we eat dinner it gets moved to the dining room.

The other way to get cool is by the air conditioner that is in the window of my parents' bedroom. Sometimes, when it is still boiling hot by bedtime, they let me put my sleeping bag on their bedroom floor. It is like camping without the annoyance of mosquitoes or the threat of bears, which I think you will agree is quite an improvement. Do they have any air conditioners at NASA? I bet it gets pretty hot in those spacesuits you astronauts have to wear. I think if I had to wear one of those, I would just die of heat prostration, which is something my mother says can happen to people and makes me wonder why adults are always so eager to send kids out into the hot sun during the summer.

Buster's family is putting in a pool, right in the ground. Sometimes we sit outside and watch the men working, digging the big hole. But Buster's mom says the pool will not be finished for quite some time. If you ask me, they should have started this project earlier. It would be nice to have cool water to jump into on a hot day like today.

If we are lucky, in the afternoon Buster's mom will let us turn on the garden hose and spray each other. But for now, on my way over to Buster's house, which is where we spend most of our days, it is just hot, hot, hot.

When I knock on the door, Mrs. Whitaker opens it and says, "Hi, Mamie."

Mrs. Whitaker is Buster's mom. Instead of Bermuda shorts, Mrs. Whitaker favors harem pants and hot pants, and I don't think she's met a paisley print yet that she doesn't like. Instead of pearls and plaids, when you see Mrs. Whitaker what you get are pinks and greens and oranges and the occasional swirling pattern that can make a person feel dizzy. I know all the ladies like my mom go to the salon to get their hair done, and Mrs. Whitaker does, too—the salon is called André's—but no one's hair looks like Mrs. Whitaker's. It is black, just like Buster's, but hers is high and poofy except for the very ends, which flip upward. It is called a bouffant hairdo. My mom sometimes wears one, but Mrs. Whitaker's is the bouffantiest and my mom says no one should wear her hair teased up as high as Mrs. Whitaker does. My mom says it is tacky. Between you and me, though? I like it.

Then there is the question of her makeup. My dad says only Cleopatra should wear eye makeup like Cleopatra, and don't get him started on the white lipstick. My dad says that Mrs. Whitaker dresses like she thinks she's still a teenager, and that even teenagers shouldn't wear the things Mrs. Whitaker does, but she has always been only kind in the years I've known her, and that is good enough for me.

Buster has a dad, too, but we don't see much of him. He commutes to work. Before Buster's bedtime got changed to nine-thirty on school nights, most nights Buster's dad got home so late, Buster wouldn't see him at all. He told me that on the weekends, his dad would look at him over his coffee at the breakfast table and say, "Who are you again?"

"Hello, Mrs. Whitaker," I say now, returning her greeting. "Is Buster up yet?"

"He sure is." She holds open the screen door for me. "You know where to find him."

"Thank you, ma'am," I say as I pass her, hearing the door shut behind me as I race down the stairs to the basement. It has a linoleum floor that stays cool no matter how hot it is outside. Because of that, it is like square tiles of heaven. And it is where Buster and I can almost always be found in the summer until we get kicked outside by his mom.

"Whatcha doing?" I ask Buster.

"Reading."

This is hardly a surprise. Buster is lying on the linoleum, his back against a cushion he's pulled from the ratty old couch, and there is a book propped up on his stomach. It's hardly a surprise because Buster is almost always reading a book.

Buster says that everything that has ever happened in the world and anything a person could ever want to know about the world can be found in books.

Even though I'm itching for the day to get started, I wait patiently as Buster finishes his page. Since he's my best friend, I know all his habits, and I know he hates to put aside a book before he's finished the page he's on. Me, I don't mind if I have to put the bookmark in if I'm only halfway down the page, or even seven-eighths. But

Buster? If the doorbell rings and he's in the middle of a page and his mother yells, "Buster, can you get that, please? My hands are all greasy from ground beef," Buster will get up from wherever he's sitting, nose still in the book, never once tearing his eyes from the words, and go open the door. I know because I have seen this for myself. I have tried to impress upon him how reckless his behavior is. He doesn't even look out the side window first. How does he know that whoever he's letting into his house isn't some kind of criminal? But that doesn't bother Buster. Buster's just going to do what Buster's going to do.

Aside from regular books, Buster is also a huge fan of comic books, Batman and Superman in particular. I think if Buster had to make a choice between being able to have his own utility belt with items like a bat-shaped grappling hook and cable strong enough to help you climb the side of a skyscraper or being faster than a speeding bullet and more powerful than a locomotive and able to leap tall buildings with a single bound, that would be a very hard choice for Buster to make.

When Buster's at a good place to set his book aside, he looks up, and that's when I get to see his eyes, which are just the right shade of brown.

"What do you want to do today?" he asks.

I shrug. "I don't know."

"We could ride our bikes to the library," Buster says.

The library is pretty much Buster's favorite place in the whole entire universe.

I shake my head hard to show I mean business. "Too hot," I say.

"We could stay down here and play with Matchbox cars," Buster says.

I shrug again. "Okay."

So that's what we do. We play with Matchbox cars until midmorning when Mrs. Whitaker yells from upstairs for us to "Come have some Hi-C!" When we get upstairs, her back is to us and she is standing at the door, peering out into the yard with one hand over her eyes like a visor against the sun. We startle her and she turns.

"Oh! I thought you kids were outside!"

So of course, after the Hi-C, that is where she tells us we need to go.

We lie under the biggest shade tree they've got, the grass underneath it scratching at any exposed skin. We watch the men work on the pool. We talk about life. Buster brings his book. Sometimes he reads quietly to himself, while I keep watching the men and thinking my thoughts.

Other times, he reads the good parts out loud to me. I do think I'd like the good parts better if I knew what the story was. We do these things until we're called for lunch—often peanut butter and jelly, although today it is bologna and mayo—and we do them after lunch, too.

On a typical day, if we are patient enough, eventually Mrs. Whitaker will call, "What are you kids doing outside? It's too hot out there." Then she will let us come in and watch TV. We watch game shows. And if *Superman* is on anywhere, of course we watch that, even though it is an old show and therefore in black-and-white, unlike *Batman*, which of course as I'm sure you know comes in color. I only know this from Buster's TV since ours is still only black-and-white. I'll bet you have a color TV, being an astronaut and all.

Sometimes Mrs. Whitaker sits with us, and then we watch *As the World Turns* or another of what she calls "my stories," which is just a fancy way to say soap operas. My mom says they rot your brain, but so far my brain's still feeling pretty good. When Michael and Claire on *As the World Turns* got divorced and Michael said he'd remarry her but then gave her his condition, which I did not quite understand because I don't get to see every episode, and *then* Claire stabbed him with a letter opener? I tell you, I thought I was going to fall out of my chair. If I'd been Claire, I'd have simply said, "No thank you." Some of the things these characters get up to in Mrs. Whitaker's stories, you do not want to know.

We do this until my mother calls to say it's time for dinner. After dinner, I go over to get Buster and it's back outside again. Buster and I can hear the kids playing elsewhere in the neighborhood, playing loudly as the mosquitoes come out to feast. I suspect they play games like hide-and-seek, kick the can, and spud. I do not care for these games. As my mother has said, speed is not my forte.

When the mosquitoes are too thick, we each go home and get ready for bed.

And that is what a typical summer day with Buster is like.

Do you see what I did there, Michael Collins? I told all that in the present tense, or as best I could, so you would feel like you were there and it was happening right now. Did it work?

Sincerely yours,
Mamie

Dear Michael Collins,

I know I said Buster was the last important person in my life you needed to know about, but right after I put my letter to you in an envelope and attached the Plant for More Beautiful Parks stamp to it—do you like the stamp? I thought it was very pretty—and I put it in our mailbox, I wanted to hit myself on the head. How could I be so stupid?

The last, the very last important "person" in my life is my cat, Campbell, who I have had for three years, since kittenhood. Someone was giving away free kittens from a box outside the A&P, and Campbell was the only one left. Campbell is named after my favorite soup brand and is a girl, but she doesn't mind having what some think of as a boy's name. We both think it's original and quite elegant.

Campbell is also not ever supposed to go outside, unless I carry her, because she is an indoor cat. Occasionally, she gets away, but she never stays gone for much more than an hour. Lately she's been getting fat, which makes me wonder: Maybe she's not getting enough exercise?

That's it.

Now you know everybody.

Also, this letter fits in the envelope just fine, but that last one about Buster? It was so long, I was barely able to get the envelope to close, even after I folded all the pages as small as I could make them. I got some other envelopes from my mom's desk, the larger envelopes that people send business material in, like contracts and things. You know, just in case I write another long letter.

At some point, if this keeps up, I may need to walk into town to the post office to get more supplies. You may think I'm too young to walk "into town," but it is not too many blocks away, we don't get all that much traffic in our town, and my mom says any exercise can only do me good. I had to wait until I turned ten to gain this privilege, and I am very proud of it. Mostly, I walk with Buster, just to be extra safe, but if I do need to go to the post office, I will find a way to go alone. For some reason, I feel like these letters should be just between us. I hope that is okay.

Sincerely yours,

Mamie

Dear Michael Collins,

I finally figured out why you never write back. Can you figure out how I figured this out? If not, I will tell you. I did the math.

Okay, I didn't really do the math, since I don't have all the information. But it struck me that I might not be the only person writing to you. I thought, if every school in the country has just one class that is writing letters to the astronauts and if in each class there is just one kid like me writing to you, then that is still a *lot* of mail.

It's no wonder you can't write back to everyone. And of course you do have other things to do right now.

I'm not sure how I feel about the idea of you getting more mail than I originally thought you did. On the one hand, I'm really happy for you. I'm glad you've got more than just me. On the other hand, it was kind of nice when I thought I was the only one. It felt special. Like I was the only one who knew about you. Which of course isn't true. The whole world knows about you. It's just that most of them don't seem to appreciate you very much.

Does it ever bother you that Neil Armstrong and Buzz Aldrin get so much more mail than you do? I hope not. It certainly wouldn't bother me. There was a time I thought it might be nice to be popular—you know, to have a lot of friends. But then Buster came along, and then Campbell, and I realized that that is quite enough for me.

Of course, I used to wonder why I didn't have a lot of friends, but I didn't have an answer for it. Now I think it might have something to do with that question Mrs. Collins my teacher asked us, about what we want to be when we grow up and how the boys said they want to be astronauts and the girls said they want to marry astronauts and I said I didn't know. And I don't. So maybe that's why I'm not more popular: because other people always seem so sure of what they want and where they're going and I just never seem to know.

I've also been wondering something else about you.

Does it ever bother you, that whole thing about how Neil Armstrong and Buzz Aldrin are going to get to walk on the moon but you won't, at least not this trip?

Okay, that's the last time I'm going to ask that question. I won't bring it up again. My lips are sealed.

Sincerely yours,
Mamie

Dear Michael Collins,

I hope you won't take this poorly, but my dad is not a fan of yours. You shouldn't mind, though. He's not a fan of Neil Armstrong or Buzz Aldrin either. As a matter of fact, he's not a fan of NASA and the entire space program. Or President Nixon.

This subject came up yet again last night at dinner.

There we sat: me, my mom, my dad, and Bess.

My mom had made the best dish in the world: chicken smothered in Campbell's cream of mushroom soup and then baked in the oven. Does Mrs. Collins your wife ever make that for you? I hope she does and, if so, you know what I'm talking about: M'm! M'm! Good!

Before getting to that, though, we had to eat the salad course first, which consisted of iceberg lettuce, tomatoes from our garden, and green goddess salad dressing. If there's enough dressing on the other stuff, I barely even notice how much I don't like them. Does Mrs. Collins serve you salad with green goddess? I hope she does. Green goddess is one of the wonders of nature.

I'd barely finished my salad and taken a first bite of chicken when trouble started.

"What's that new TV set doing in the living room?" my dad asked.

Uh-oh. It's not like I couldn't have seen this coming—anyone could—but still. Uh-oh.

"I didn't think I needed your permission before making a purchase for the home," my mom said.

"No one said you did," my dad said. "But when a man comes home from a hard day at work and there's a new television set replacing the perfectly good old one, I think he has a right to ask about it."

Whenever my dad starts talking about himself in the third person—"a man" and "he" instead of the usual "I"—it's plain to see that no good can come of it.

"I just thought it'd be nice for us to join the modern era," my mom said. "You know, replace the old black-and-white with color."

If it were up to me to be the judge of this one, I'd have to come down on my mom's side. I'd seen that color TV in the living room, a great big Magnavox even bigger than the Whitakers', as soon as I'd come home from Buster's house and I was itching to get my fingers on the knobs.

"Why now?" my dad asked.

"Pardon me?" my mom said.

"Why now?" he said again. "Why, exactly, do we need color at this moment in time?"

"Why, to watch the space launch next week, of course," my mom said, "and then to watch the astronauts walk on the moon."

My dad pointed the business end of his fork at her. "And that right there is what's wrong with this country."

"Color television sets?" my mom said, playing dumb.

We all knew what my dad was getting at. We'd all heard versions of it before.

"I suppose you'd like to watch the space launch in color, too, Mamie?" my dad asked, delaying the inevitable.

"I guess it could be nice," I said quietly, staring at my plate of chicken.

"And how about you, Bess?" my dad asked. "What do you have to say about all this?"

At the sound of her name, Bess looked up. "I'm sorry," she said. "What did you say?"

"Useless," was my dad's response. "You might as well *be* on the moon for all the attention you pay to what goes on in this house these days."

We knew what he meant by that, too. Ever since Bess started dating Vinny, he's been the only thing she can think or talk about. Everything is "Vinny this" and "Vinny that."

My father is not a huge fan of Vinny's. My father says that Vinny's hair is too long. My father says that only Jesus should look like Jesus.

"Billions of dollars!" my dad practically shouted. And here it was. The inevitable had finally arrived.

"Billions of taxpayer dollars this country is spending to put a man on the moon," he continued. "And for what? So we can win the space race? So we can outdo the Russians? Why?"

He looked like he would've liked an answer, but none of us were about to try giving him one. We knew that whatever we said it'd be wrong.

"Nixon thinks he's so smart," my dad muttered. "But tell me this: Who *cares* who wins the space race?"

Just about everybody, I thought to myself.

But then I started to wonder: Do you care about the space race, Michael Collins? Is it something you think about? Like when you get up in the morning, is your first thought, *I hope we win this space race thing—we need to beat those Russians to the moon?*

"Nixon didn't start the space race," my mom pointed out.

"No, he didn't." My dad let her have the point. "Kennedy did. But it's Nixon who's determined to finish it."

The table fell silent just long enough for me to take another bite of chicken. I must confess, even with the cream of mushroom soup, it was less "M'm! M'm! Good!" than usual.

"At least Nixon said twenty-five thousand troops will leave Vietnam by the end of August," my mom pointed out hopefully.

"But we never should have been there in the first place," my dad shot back.

"True," my mom agreed.

My parents have very strong feelings about politics, some of which they agree on.

My dad will say, "You can't blame blacks for rioting in the streets. You can't oppress people forever and expect anything different. If the situation were reversed, whites would be doing the exact same thing," to which my mom always agrees. But then my mom will sometimes add, "Maybe women should riot in the streets, too?" When she says those words, my dad never has anything to say and his lips tighten in a thin line.

"What does it even mean?" my dad went on. "So one country wins the space race. Big deal. If the two countries are on the brink of war later, do you think the country that loses the space race will suddenly say, 'Oh, I'm sorry. My mistake. You're so much better than we are because you won the space race. We can't possibly fight with you. We'd only lose.' Of course not. Any future wars, and how they resolve themselves, will boil down to what it always has: who has the bigger army; who has the better weapons; who has the largest, most dedicated, and best trained fighting force." He threw down his napkin in disgust. "But it won't have a thing to do with who walks on the moon first."

I don't know much about war, outside of what I hear my parents say or what Mrs. Collins my teacher said in class about Vietnam, so I had no idea if anything my dad was saying was right or wrong, but I'll tell you this, Michael Collins: I kind of admired the force with which he made his argument. There's something about a person believing strongly in something that's more appealing than believing in nothing.

"And what good is Apollo 11?" my dad said. "The dang thing isn't even reusable!"

I didn't understand what he meant by that, about it not being reusable, but then he said, "They won't be happy until they have another disaster on their hands."

Now this was new. This had never been part of any of my dad's speeches before, so I couldn't help but ask, "Disaster?"

"Grissom, White, and Chaffee," my dad said. "Three astronauts who burned to death in an earlier Apollo ship."

"They died of smoke inhalation," my mom corrected. "That's what the reports said."

"Doesn't matter." My dad shrugged. "Dead is dead. Poor fools never even left the Earth. This is what this country is spending billions of taxpayer dollars for? When we've already got plenty of other problems that money could be used for right here on Earth?"

I'm sure he said a lot more things, but I barely heard those last words and I definitely didn't hear anything that came anywhere near immediately afterward because my mind had frozen at "Three astronauts who burned to death in an earlier Apollo ship."

Is that true, Michael Collins? Did you know about this? Did you know about this before saying that, yes, you'd go on this mission? Did you know the risk, and still you said yes?

My mind wasn't just stopped at these words. My mind was screaming now.

DID YOU KNOW YOU COULD DIE, MICHAEL COLLINS?

It took a while for the roaring in my head to quiet down. By then, my mom was saying something about how she thought it would be nice for us to have a Launch Party, invite people over so we can all watch together, and my dad was saying, "Over my dead body."

A party, even the idea of one, would normally be such an exciting thing. We hardly ever have parties, unless it's someone's birthday. Even the Fourth of July, it's mostly just red Jell-O served next to a white cake with frosting dyed blue and maybe a sparkler, which is exactly what we did this year. Exciting as that is, you can't really call it a party.

But even the idea of a party with more than a fancy cake and a sparkler involved couldn't cheer me, because if it was no longer roaring, my mind was still whispering:

Did you know, Michael Collins? Did you know?

Sincerely yours,
Mamie

Dear Michael Collins,

The worst has happened.

Someone knows about us.

Today, Buster and I were playing outside my house in the afternoon when Bess flew through the door, laughing and waving some sheets of paper in the air.

We were playing at my house because today is Wednesday and Wednesday is Mrs. Whitaker's big cleaning day. She doesn't like us underfoot when she's doing that. And we don't particularly like being underfoot on those days either. Because if we are, there's just no telling what we might be drafted into doing.

I recognized those sheets of paper, and I knew it spelled doom to life as I've known it.

It was my most recent letter to you, which I had yet to mail because it was late when I finished writing last night, so I'd left it on the desk in my bedroom.

"What were you doing in my bedroom?" I asked.

"You've been writing to Michael Collins?" Bess asked,

barely able to contain her laughter as she ignored my question. That laughter, it was like being Charlie Brown in *Peanuts* all over again: HA! HA! HA! HA! HA! HA! *HA!* "And you actually believe he'll write you back?"

I would like to think there's a good reason why an older sister would torture a younger one. But in my experience, at least when it comes to Bess, it strictly boils down to opportunity and a few spare minutes of time on her hands.

"You've been writing to Michael Collins?" Buster echoed, looking some combination of surprised and hurt before I had the chance to answer. "The astronaut?"

"Yes," I said, snatching at the pages, which Bess held out of reach. "Yes, the astronaut."

"What is this, Mamie?" Bess asked.

"It's just a stupid school assignment," I said, jumping to try to grab back those pages.

I started to jump so hard and so frequently, I could feel the sweat breaking out all across my forehead. After this was over with, I just might need to ask permission to get the hose out early.

"Everyone was supposed to write to an astronaut, and I picked him," I said.

"Only you, Mamie," Bess said.

I must confess, her words made me wonder: *What did she mean by that?*

"And in case you haven't noticed," Bess went on, "it's summer vacation. So how can *this* be a school assignment?"

"I didn't finish it in time," I said, flustered. "You don't want me to get an F, do you?"

"And what are you doing telling him all kinds of things about our family?" she said.

"Well," I defended myself like Perry Mason, "I had to write *something*."

"I repeat, it's summer, so this can't be a school assignment." She paused. "Maybe there *was* an assignment, in the beginning . . ."

This time, I kept my arms crossed against my chest and my mouth shut. If I didn't say anything, no evidence could be used against me in a court of law. And anyway, how could I tell anyone, how could I ever explain to another human being so that they'd understand that what had started out as a stupid school assignment had somehow turned into something I now wanted and needed to do somewhat regularly?

Then a gleam came into Bess's eye. "You like him!"

"Do not!"

"You love him. You're in love with Michael Collins!"

"AM NOT!"

"And the really funny thing is, you probably actually believe he's reading these things."

"Just give me my sheets of paper, please," I said firmly, holding out my hand.

"Fine." Bess handed them back so quickly I had to grab them fast before they scattered to kingdom come. "But don't be thinking that he's ever going to write you. And really, Mamie. Of all the astronauts to pick? *Michael Collins?*"

"It's not like there is an 'of all the astronauts to pick,'" I objected. "There's only three!"

But she didn't answer. She was already walking away, laughing again.

It was so silent after she left, I could practically hear the sweat drying on my forehead. It was Buster who finally spoke first.

"You've been writing to Michael Collins?" he said again. "The astronaut?"

"Yes," I admitted again.

Another long silence, then:

"I'm sorry, Mamie," Buster said. "I've got to go."

And he went.

Sincerely yours,
Mamie

Dear Michael Collins,

Today I got up, got dressed, brushed my teeth, went downstairs, remembered to feed Campbell, had Cap'n Crunch but not Froot Loops. When I was finished, I just sat there at the table.

"Aren't you going to ask if you can go over Buster's house?" my mom asked.

"Maybe not today," I said.

"What's wrong?" she asked. "Are you sick?"

Well, of course I was sick. Sick to my stomach that my best friend now knew the secret I'd been keeping: that I've been writing to you. Sick to my stomach that based on the look on his face and the way he left so quickly, in the middle of the afternoon and with so many hours of daylight remaining, that my best friend wasn't even my best friend anymore. Was it because I'd kept it a secret from him? Was it because he thought that what I was doing was dumb? If it was the first reason, I could try to apologize at least. But if it was the second, I didn't see how either of us could ever get over that.

My mom put her hand to my forehead.

"You don't feel warm," she said. Then she looked at my empty bowl. "And you haven't lost your appetite."

Oh, the betrayal of still being able to eat. But just because I was sick to my stomach and felt like I could die, it didn't mean I wanted to starve.

"Did you and Buster have a fight?" she asked.

"No, ma'am," I said, which was only the truth. We hadn't fought. Buster and I have never fought.

"You didn't go over there last night like you usually do," she said.

To this, I said nothing. What could I say?

"You go on over there now. I have things to do today."

"Yes, ma'am."

Walking over, though, I took the long way. By this I mean I walked heel to toe at the pace of one step every half minute, also making figure-eight loops between the line of trees separating our property from the Whitakers', so by the time I got to Buster's front door it was well past the time I'd normally arrive.

Why was I so scared to go there? Because for the first time ever, I didn't want to see Buster. I didn't want to see the kind of look on his face that other kids at school sometimes gave me, the kind of look my own sister Bess had given me yesterday. I didn't want to see the kind of look that would say that I was just worthless and that he was no longer my friend.

At the door, I pressed the bell as lightly as I could, hoping no one would hear me and then I could just go away. But in no time, Mrs. Whitaker was there, with her Cleopatra eyes and hoop earrings so big that when she tilted her head just the slightest bit, the bottom of one of the hoops grazed the top of her shoulder.

"You're late," she said, sounding surprised by that fact.

Before we could go into our routine of her saying hi, then me saying hi and asking if Buster could play, and her telling me to go downstairs—which I had no stomach for, for reasons already expressed—she opened the door wide.

"Well, come on in," she continued. "Buster's been waiting for you. In fact, he's been waiting so loudly, he's driving me crazy."

I had no idea what she could mean by that. All I could do was step inside and go downstairs like it was any other summer day, even while it felt like the exact opposite of that.

I wanted to walk down those stairs as slowly as possible, like I'd done with the trees. But I could feel Mrs. Whitaker's eyes on my back—it was like those eyes were saying, *Well, go on, then*—and I was therefore forced to proceed at a normal pace.

At the bottom of the stairs, I looked across the basement and there was Buster, not reading.

Someone had set up a card table, and on top of it Buster was making something with all the colors of Play-Doh.

When Buster's engrossed in something, even if that something is not any kind of reading material, it can be difficult to get his attention. But he must've heard me, because as I got near the table, he looked up.

"Mamie!"

"What's that?" I asked, pointing at the Play-Doh.

"It's Apollo 11," he said.

"Impressive," I said.

I must confess, though, Michael Collins, I didn't have the heart to tell him that it was *hardly* impressive. But lots of times, when you're working with Play-Doh, it really has more to do with the imagination than what is actually in front of you.

"Nah." Buster waved a hand, laughing at himself. "I know it's not."

"It's colorful at least," I tried again.

"Well, yeah, it's that." Buster laughed some more. "But we can do better."

"We?"

"Look what I found," he said. Then he pulled out a magazine and turned to a page. On it was an ad for:

APOLLO-SATURN ROCKET

stands 4 feet high

—amazingly detailed right down

to capsule hatch doors

KIT INCLUDES:

escape tower

command module

service module

lunar module

and all three stages of Saturn V, plus base

$10.49

"We're going to build *that*?" I said, not even knowing what half the words in the ad meant. What are a command module and a service module and a lunar module? And why would a person need three different modules anyway? But I tell you, the picture accompanying the ad was impressive, the rocket nearly as tall as the boy standing next to it.

"Well, no," Buster said. "I just found the ad last night. By the time we sent away for it and it got back to us, it'd be weeks from now. But we can definitely do better than the Play-Doh one."

That's when he pulled out his Erector set.

Do you know what an Erector set is, Michael Collins? It is all these metal bars of different sizes that have holes in the middle, and you put the pieces together using screws and bolts to construct things. It is a marvelous invention, enjoyed by boys everywhere—and many girls, too.

"You want to build an Apollo 11 out of your Erector set with me," I said flatly. Do you know how that happens, Michael Collins? How sometimes you're so shocked by a turn of events, your voice just goes flat? It's like there's so much emotion, there's no emotion.

"Well, yeah," Buster said. "And afterward, when we're

done, we can take our bikes to the library. Or if it's late when we finish this, we'll go tomorrow."

"What are we going to do there?"

"Research. Read things, of course. Find out more about Apollo 11."

"But wait," I said. "You've never cared about the space race before."

"I did," Buster said. "But I thought you weren't interested, so I didn't talk about it. Now that I know you are, too, I'm even more interested." He shrugged. "If it's important to you, it's important to me."

"Then you weren't mad at me," I said, still feeling some of that fear, "when you left yesterday?"

"Oh, I was mad," he said. "But then last night, I realized I was only mad because I felt hurt—hurt that you hadn't shared it with me when we always share just about everything. But then I saw how dumb that was—you must've had your reasons—and I immediately thought how great it is that you're so interested in the same thing I'm interested in." He shrugged. "Plus, like I said, if it's important to you, it's important to me."

I have to tell you, Michael Collins. There is not much in this world that makes me want to cry, but as Buster opened the box for the Erector set, as we began constructing our own version of Apollo 11, my eyes were swimming.

And when we were done? That thing we'd constructed together looked *nothing* like the $10.49 Apollo-Saturn rocket toy we'd seen in the ad, but that did not matter, not one bit, because nothing I'd ever seen in my whole life had ever looked so beautiful.

Nothing.

Sincerely yours,
Mamie

Dear Michael Collins,

Is there any place you're scared to go? I know you're not scared of going into space—which I would certainly be scared to do—in something my dad refers to as "a tin can" because otherwise you wouldn't be doing it. But isn't there someplace in the world that does scare you?

I will let you in on a little secret that no one else knows about me. Before today, I was scared of the library. There are all those books, so many that I practically never know where to start. Plus, I worry that the librarian will laugh at my selections or, if not laugh, give me the kind of look that will make me feel dumb. It's not really anything that's ever happened there. It's just how I feel. Overwhelmed.

Of course Buster wants to go there all the time, but this isn't about him. My mother goes to the library every single week to get new books for her and my dad, and sometimes she has me go with her and then I get books, too. My parents are both big readers. In fact, everyone in my family is a big reader. I'm not sure how much reading Eleanor's doing since she moved out. And Bess isn't so much anymore, not since she started dating Vinny. But before that? From the time I was real little, Sunday excitement at my house was, after church and Sunday dinner, my dad lying down on the couch going one way, my mom lying down on the couch going the other, Bess and Eleanor taking comfy chairs and me lying down on my stomach on the floor. What was everyone doing? Reading. Since they all did it, I felt like I should do it, too.

But here is the thing. They all turn the pages so quickly. One time, I measured this. At the top of the hour, my mom was on page forty-seven of her book. And when I checked again over her shoulder, after the minute hand had made a full sweep of the clock? She was on page ninety-seven. *Ninety-seven*, Michael Collins! In just one single hour, the woman had read *fifty whole pages*! There's no way I could compete with that, no way I could compete with any of them. So I would turn the pages of my book, not as fast as they did, but more quickly than I could possibly read them, so that they would think I could sort of keep up and was not just some slow person who'd been accidentally dropped into the wrong house.

Sometimes—again, when I was little—I would use

this technique in school. Like when the teacher would have us read a chapter quietly to ourselves. At school, I am what is known as a slow reader. There I'd be, reading at my own pace and still pages from the end of the chapter, and there everyone else would be, all done. So I learned to skim, sometimes turning pages without reading what was on them, just so I wouldn't be last. It's hard being last at a thing because when you finally finish and look up, everyone else is looking back at you as if to say, *Why are you so slow?* and *We are getting tired of waiting for you.* Of course, it is also not easy to answer questions about the story when you have not read all the words.

One day, though, Bess caught me. This was last year. Earlier in the week my mom had made me go with her to the library to get a book. I picked a Nancy Drew mystery, *The Password to Larkspur Lane*, because I liked the title and the cover. So there I was on the floor, doing what I usually did with books, when Bess said, "You're not even reading that!"

"Am too," I said, looking at the page number I'd managed to flip to. "I'm on page fourteen—says so right here."

"Fine." She snatched the book away from me. "Then tell me what the story is about."

I thought about this, remembering the title. "It's

about a street called Larkspur Lane." I paused. "And there's a password involved."

Surprisingly, Bess didn't say anything about that. She just flipped the pages back until she got to the first one and then she placed the book on the floor in front of me, open.

"Start at the beginning, Mamie," she said, "and read all the words. This isn't a contest here."

I looked up to see if my parents or Eleanor would have anything to say about this. Not only was I not as quick a reader as everyone else, but now I'd also been exposed as being a cheat-reader. Thankfully, their noses were still buried in their own books and they hadn't noticed a thing.

With no other choice, since Bess was staring at me, I began to read the story again, every single word and at my own pace. And you know something? That book was good! If you ever need something entertaining to take your mind off things, Michael Collins, you could do worse than Nancy Drew, which I highly recommend.

Right then and there, I vowed to myself never to be a cheat-reader again. I realized that doing things the way I'd been doing them before, not only was it wrong, but I was also running the risk of missing out on some of the good stuff—even if it made me the last one to finish reading at school.

But even though I liked the Nancy Drew mystery, I was still scared of the library. Given my past—the shame of being exposed as a cheat-reader at a young age, even though I am no longer one and never will be again; feeling bad at school for being a slow reader—it is a lot for one person to overcome. And being in a library? Surrounded by wall-to-wall books? It can bring those feelings all crashing back. Who knows where fear comes from? It doesn't always make sense.

But here is what I discovered today. The library? It is a *spectacular* place! If you go there because there is something you really want to know about, then Buster is right, it can be pretty much the most amazing place in the world.

Before today, I would only go with Buster as a favor to him, because that is what you do if you're lucky enough to have a good friend: sometimes, you do what they want to do, simply because they want to do it.

But today?

Buster strode right up to the front desk and said, "Hello, Miss Penny." He said it to her like she was a close acquaintance, just like he always does.

"Hello, Buster," she said. Her glasses slid down her

nose and then she peered at me over the tops. "I see you have Mamie with you today."

"Yes, ma'am," Buster said. "We were wondering if you could help us."

"I can certainly try," Miss Penny said.

I immediately liked that about her. She didn't outright offer any guarantees, but at least she was willing to make the effort. It made me wonder some why I'd never asked for her help picking out books before. Maybe in the past, I should've just given her a chance to do her job.

"I would like," Buster said, "to see anything that you have on rocket ships. Specifically, I'd like anything on Apollo 11."

Miss Penny, finger tapping against lip as she considered our request, took her glasses the rest of the way off her nose and dropped them. I figured it was a good thing she had her glasses attached to a string of beads that ran around her neck. Otherwise, that would be a very dangerous thing to do with eyeglasses.

"I think our best bet would be periodicals," Miss Penny said.

I liked that she used the word "our," too. It made me feel like we were all in this together.

"Why don't you and Mamie take a seat at the table

over there," Miss Penny suggested, "and I'll see what I can find."

Our bottoms had barely touched the chairs when Buster called after her, "And Michael Collins! Bring anything you can find on Michael Collins, too!"

Miss Penny stopped and turned.

"Not Neil Armstrong?" she asked.

Buster shook his head.

"Not Buzz Aldrin?" Miss Penny asked.

"No, ma'am." Buster shook his head again. "We'd like to see what you've got on Michael Collins. You know, he's the best one."

Once her back was turned again, Buster looked over at me and grinned, and I grinned right back. How could I not?

When Miss Penny returned, her arms were filled with the periodicals she'd promised us, all kinds of newspapers and magazines.

As Buster began reading to himself about rocket ships and Apollo 11, I began reading about you.

And let me tell you something, Michael Collins, that you may not know about yourself: there is a *lot* more to you than meets the eye.

You are thirty-eight years old and you were born in

Rome, which is in Italy. *Rome*, in *Italy*! Your birthday is Halloween. Isn't that something? I know there must be people born every day of the year, even November 22, the day President Kennedy was assassinated. Even though I was only four at the time, I still remember the sadness in our house that day with my older sisters and my mom crying and even my dad's eyes getting wet when he came home early from work. That must be a tough day to have a birthday, because the country has not stopped being sad about him dying. But I have to say, I've never known of anyone who was born on Halloween before. That must be quite a thing.

The reason you were born in Rome is because your father was stationed over there with the U.S. Army. Because of your father's work, you moved around a lot. Before you were even eighteen, you'd lived in Oklahoma, New York, Puerto Rico, Texas, and Virginia. Wow, Michael Collins. I've only ever lived in one place before, and that place is right here in Connecticut, which you have probably figured out from my return address.

Instead of doing what your mom wanted you to do, which was go into the diplomatic service, you decided to do what your father did and join the military. Seventeen years ago, you graduated 185th at the United States

Military Academy from a total of 527 cadets in your class. I hope you don't mind me saying this, Michael Collins, but I was a bit surprised at that. I would have thought someone selected to go to the moon on Apollo 11 would have done somewhat better in school. I would've thought you'd have graduated much higher in your class. Like first. Or at least third. On the other hand, it gives me hope. If someone like you who did mediocre in school could still get so far in life, then perhaps there is still hope for a slow reader and onetime cheat-reader like me. Was reading a problem for you, too? I suspect not. I suspect you may have had other challenges, as do we all, challenges that kept you at 185th.

You once had to eject from an F-86 plane because of a fire near the cockpit. Were you scared? I would've been. Fire, to me, seems a good reason not to do a thing again if you are lucky enough to survive. And yet even after that, you remained a pilot.

After seeing what John Glenn did on the Mercury Atlas 6, you decided to become an astronaut, too. You did not get accepted into the NASA program right away, and yet you just kept on trying. Over a year after first trying, you were accepted.

You have gone into space once already, on Gemini

10, and you even got to stick your head out of the hatch. That must have purely been something, much better than riding in your basic convertible, which I have yet to have had the thrill of experiencing for myself.

It was you who had to tell Martha Chaffee that her husband, Roger, died in Apollo 1 along with Gus Grissom and Ed White. I bet that was even harder than ejecting from an F-86 because of a fire near the cockpit.

Last year, you had to have surgery to fix a physical problem and you had to spend the three months afterward in a neck brace. This meant you couldn't go on Apollo 9, as had been planned. After the fire and everything else you went through, I'd have been relieved to have an excuse to stay right here on Earth, where it is so much safer. But I suspect you did not feel that way. If you did, you wouldn't be planning to go into space again.

Because of your previous space flight experience, you were selected just this January, along with Neil Armstrong and Edwin "Buzz" Aldrin, Jr., for Apollo 11.

Wow, Michael Collins, just wow. From 185th in your class to this.

Your wife's first name is Patricia, but people like to call her Pat, just like our First Lady. I had to laugh when I read that, because at first I wondered if Mrs. Collins your wife was named after a First Lady, just like my parents named me and my sisters. But then I had to laugh even more, this time at myself, when I realized that of course this couldn't possibly be true.

You have a daughter, Kate, who was born the same year as me, as well as two other children.

I wonder what all this must be like for Kate. If she is excited. Or scared. I can't even begin to imagine what it must feel like having her dad go off one day to do something and not knowing if he will ever come back. I also wonder: Is it hard for you to leave her? Is it hard for her to let you go?

I do realize that you already know these things about yourself. But let me tell you, it was news to me. I suspect that this would also be news to all those people who think Neil Armstrong and Buzz Aldrin are the best ones. I further suspect that, sooner rather than later, Buster will tell me everything he learned about rocket ships and Apollo 11 today.

Sincerely yours,
Mamie

Dear Michael Collins,

"Holy moly!"

That would be Buster saying that. "Holy moly!" is Buster's absolute favorite thing in the world to say when he is excited about something, and if you haven't come across those two words before in my letters to you, that's only because Buster hasn't had anything to go "Holy moly!" about until now.

I know you must be getting busier and busier preparing for the trip. But if you read my last letter, then you may recall I promised that Buster would likely tell me everything he learned about rocket ships and Apollo 11 sooner rather than later.

Well, sooner is now.

When I arrived at Buster's this morning, instead of Mrs. Whitaker answering the door, it was him. He looked like he hadn't even bothered to take the time to comb his hair—he was that excited for me to arrive, practically yanking my arm off as he pulled me into the house and down to the basement.

He had a surprise waiting for me. Two, actually.

The first surprise was some liquid he'd poured into two glasses. The liquid was orange but by no means as thick as orange juice. I must confess to being a bit scared by this turn of events. In the past, Buster has tried to cook a thing or two for me, and the results have been something less than desirable.

Buster handed me one of the two glasses and kept one for himself, from which he took a huge long glug.

"Aren't you going to try it?" he asked, wiping the back of his hand across his mouth.

"What is it?" I said, raising one eyebrow as I gazed at the contents of my glass. If you want the truth, that particular shade of orange was not inviting.

"It's Tang."

"Tang?"

"Tang! You know, like the astronauts drink? Haven't you seen the commercials?"

Figuring that if this is something you drink, Michael Collins, then it would be okay for me to drink it, too, I closed my eyes tight and glugged away. Immediately, I understood why Buster had wiped his mouth with the back of his hand, because this was not a taste a person wanted to linger over. In its defense, it *was* tangy.

I figure maybe it's the kind of thing a person needs to get used to.

Having satisfied Buster with my glug, I gave him my glass back, and he set both mine and his aside.

Then it was time for his second surprise.

"Ta-da!" he said, waving his hands toward the card table like a magician showing off a lady split in two or something.

For all his excitement, you'd have thought he'd sent away for the Apollo-Saturn rocket he'd shown me in that magazine, and had it shipped real extra quick. But no. The same Erector set version we'd worked on together still sat there, unchanged.

"I'm sorry, Buster," I said. I didn't want to hurt his feelings. "But how is that 'Ta-da!'?"

"Not that," he said. "This." And that's when he held up a bunch of papers from the table that I hadn't noticed lying there.

I still didn't want to hurt his feelings, so that time I didn't say what I was thinking, which is that a bunch of papers was even less "Ta-da!" than our Erector set model.

But my lack of any visible enthusiasm didn't dampen Buster's.

"Look!" he said. "Based on everything I read at the

library yesterday, I've drawn some illustrations, and now I can explain to you how the rocket ship works and how things are going to happen!"

Oh. *Oh!*

I figured that if I understood more about everything than I did before, then maybe I would feel less scared for you, so I pulled up a folding chair for myself, and one for him. I even took another glug of Tang, which I regretted almost instantly. Then I parked my elbows on the table and my head in my hands, preparing to be educated.

"Okay, as you know," Buster said, "Neil Armstrong is the commander, Buzz Aldrin is the lunar module pilot and Michael Collins is the command module pilot."

"Buster, I don't know any of that, except for the part about Neil Armstrong. What does that all even mean?"

"Maybe I started in the wrong spot. Here, let me explain about the rocket to you." He held up one of his illustrations, which bore a fair resemblance to pictures of rocket ships I'd seen in the news—a long cylinder with some stuff at the bottom of it and some other stuff on top.

"The whole thing," Buster said, "is three hundred and sixty-three feet tall."

I tried to imagine a height so big, and couldn't.

"Picture a thirty-story building," Buster said. "Most of it just holds rocket fuel, and the whole thing weighs six and a half *million* pounds."

Buster stopped talking and looked at me, waiting. Those sure were big numbers to grasp. But after a long minute, I nodded for him to go on.

"The long cylinder part is the Saturn V. That's the actual rocket."

"Wait. What about Apollo 11?" I said.

"The whole thing is called that, but they need names for the individual parts; otherwise, how would anyone know what anyone else is talking about? I'm sorry," he said, perhaps seeing my look of confusion. "Maybe this kind of thing is just interesting to boys."

I resented that. So I made him explain everything until I thought I mostly got it. The whole mission was called Apollo 11 and the entire ship was called that, too, but it was composed of parts: the Saturn V rocket to power it; the *Columbia*, the command/service module, where the astronauts would be for the flight and which would be the only part returning to Earth; and the *Eagle*, the lunar module, which would detach from the *Columbia*, carrying Armstrong and Aldrin down to the moon's surface and then back to the *Columbia*.

"Go on," I said.

"The Saturn V rocket fires in three stages, and you light the fuel on fire here," he said, pointing toward the base of his drawing, "and then—"

"You light the fuel on fire?" I echoed, stopping him. "That doesn't seem very bright to me." I'd seen signs at gas stations—everybody has—telling people not to throw lit matches out the window because of the gas in the tanks. If the flame met the gas, you could end up with a fire or even an explosion. And here, these people down in Cape Kennedy were going to deliberately set fuel on fire? Were they out of their minds? Are you, Michael Collins?

"It's the only way," Buster said. "With a rocket, the burning fuel creates gas. That's just how it works."

Buster stopped talking, looked at me, and waited for me to accept what he'd said. But that was hard to do, because of what I was thinking about.

"Buster, do you know about Grissom, White, and Chaffee?"

"Of course. They're the astronauts who died. Everyone knows about them."

I hadn't, not until recently.

"Could what happened to them happen to Armstrong,

Aldrin, and Michael Collins?" I was still thinking of the foolishness of deliberately setting fuel on fire.

"That was just an accident," Buster said, "an awful, horrible accident. But I'm sure that right after that happened, NASA took protective measures to make sure that same exact thing will never, *ever* happen again."

"Phew!" I actually made that noise out loud, releasing a breath I had no idea I'd been holding and yet probably had in a way ever since my dad first mentioned the names Gus Grissom, Ed White, and Roger Chaffee, and about the tragic thing that had happened to them.

"I know." Buster smiled. "It's a relief, isn't it?"

"Yes," I said, feeling the "Phew!" all over again, only this time on the inside. "The astronauts won't die."

"Oh, they could still die."

"What?"

"A million ways. Probably even a million and one. There are all *kinds* of things that could still go wrong, just not the same exact things that have gone wrong in the past."

I suppose I could've asked Buster for examples, and perhaps I should've, but frankly, right then I simply did not want to know. And so I kept mostly quiet as Buster's attention went back to his drawing.

"So after they set fire to the fuel," he said, "the Saturn V rocket lifts Apollo 11 straight up in the air and what they call Stage 1 of the rocket burns for a few minutes before falling back to Earth."

"Wait. What? They build it all, but it doesn't all go to the moon?" It made me think about what my dad said, about all the stuff not even being reusable. It also sounded dangerous.

Buster nodded and went on. "Stage 2 then ignites and it also burns, and then it's Stage 3's turn, sending Apollo 11 into orbit and propelling it toward the moon before falling away."

I spoke my fear out loud. "But isn't that dangerous? All that debris just falling down?"

"Maybe it disintegrates when it hits the atmosphere or something—I don't know." Buster shrugged. "I'm not a rocket scientist, Mamie. All I can tell you is, they've done this several times before and never had any problems. Well, except for when they've had problems."

That was hardly reassuring.

"If the three stages fall away, what's left?"

"Only everything else that's important! Like the *Columbia* and the *Eagle*. Oh, but first. See that?" Buster pointed at the top of his drawing, tapping the page. "That there is the escape tower."

"Escape tower?"

"Sure. It's on top of the *Columbia*. It has its own rocket and will separate if something goes wrong during the launch."

"That's fantastic! But wait. *Only* during the launch?"

"That's right. But if nothing goes wrong during the launch, the escape tower, like those other things I mentioned, will also jettison—that basically means it falls away—once it's no longer needed."

For a moment there, I had been relieved by the idea of an escape tower. But if you ask me, it's not much of an option if it goes away so quickly.

I tried to picture it in my mind, what it would look like: so many pieces falling away, eventually leaving a smaller part of the original to head on up to the moon.

"When they get close enough," Buster said, "Armstrong and Aldrin will get in the *Eagle* and land on the surface of the moon while Michael Collins remains with the *Columbia*, orbiting."

Now there was something I really wanted to know.

"Why does Michael Collins have to stay with the *Columbia*?" I asked. "Why can't he go down to the moon in the *Eagle* with the other two?"

Here is one of the things I love about Buster. When I asked that question, he didn't laugh at me like I was Charlie

Brown in *Peanuts*. He didn't even smile at me as if to say, *But it should be obvious to any idiot!* or *What a silly question.*

Instead, he just answered, "Because someone has to stay with the ship, keeping it on course, so that there's a ship to come back to."

I nodded. That made sense.

"Remember how I said a million, maybe even a million and one, things could go wrong?"

I nodded again.

"Well, if anything goes wrong with the moon landing, it's Michael Collins's job to still return to Earth, even if he has to do so alone."

That was too big for my brain: the other astronauts could die and it would be your job, your duty, to come home alone?

It must have been too big for Buster's brain, too, because almost immediately, he said, "But that won't happen. Of course it won't."

"You sure have learned a lot about this quickly," I said to Buster, because it was true and also because I wanted to steer the subject away from people maybe dying or maybe having to return home alone, at least for a little while.

"You know me." Buster shrugged.

I do.

"When I become interested in a thing," he said, "I just have to learn all I can about it."

"I know," I said. "Otherwise you get headaches. But this." I indicated the table with the Play-Doh model, the Erector set model, the ad for the rocket, and all of Buster's drawings. "I know that after you first found out about me writing to Michael Collins, you said you were always interested in it but even more so once you knew I was, too. But this." I waved at the table again. "This is a bit much, even for you."

"Is it?" Buster looked around, surprised. "I don't think so. I mean, of course I'm more interested in anything once you are, too, but as soon as I got started . . ." He paused. "It's more than just that now."

"Like what? What more?"

"Holy moly, Mamie! These *men* are going *to the moon*! Do you know how incredible that is? Sometimes when I think about it, I have to make myself stop after a bit because the thoughts in my head are so amazing, I worry my mind will maybe explode!"

"But why?" I said. "Why is it so amazing to you?"

"Why?" He ran his hands back and forth through his

messy hair, making it even worse if possible, like that might help him think more clearly. "Okay, it's like this. You know how I feel about Batman and Superman, right?"

I shrugged. "You love them."

"Right. But they're not real."

"But you still love them."

"And I'll never not love them! But they're made-up superheroes. They're fiction. And fiction is great, don't get me wrong. The astronauts, though? They're real live superheroes, attempting to do the most extraordinary thing that any human being has ever attempted. And if they can pull this off? Who *knows* what people will be able to do next?"

I had to admit, when he put it like that, his excitement made perfect sense.

We sat in silence for a bit, thinking on the enormity of it all, until a thought crept back into my brain.

"But Michael Collins will get to go another time, right?" I said. "If Apollo 11 is successful, they'll let him go to the moon again and even walk on it, won't they?"

"Of course not," Buster said.

"How come?"

"There are too many other astronauts in the space program. NASA will never use him again, not for something like this. They'll send other people."

Like with the stuff I read about you in the library, I'm sure you know all of this already. But it was absolutely news to me, Michael Collins. I never realized before what it meant, how much danger you are in and how you will come so close and yet never, *ever* get to walk on the moon.

It is a lot to think about.

Sincerely yours,
Mamie

Dear Michael Collins,

Perhaps you will notice something different about this letter to you. For the first time, I have put the date at the top of it. That is because, with you set to leave Earth tomorrow, it seems important to record the days and sometimes even the hours and the minutes.

You may have noticed something else, too. This is the first time I have written to you in several days. I have been keeping silent because, with your important mission ahead, I did not want to be a distraction. But since I know that any letter I write to you today, or any letters I may write to you in the week or so to follow, won't reach you until after you've survived the journey, which I hope does happen, I feel free to write once more.

I have also been busy the past several days. What I have been doing is playing "astronauts" with Buster and drinking Tang. Astronauts is a game we made up in which we are the Apollo 11 crew, heading off to the moon. In the game, Buster is Neil Armstrong and I am you. Since we don't have another neighborhood friend, what to do about Buzz Aldrin presented a bit of a problem. At first we were going to use one of my old stuffed animals—I thought the giraffe would make a good choice—but then Buster got the idea to have my cat do it. So Campbell is our Buzz. I carry her over to Buster's house. Or, if we get kicked outside, we provide close supervision of the cat. I must say, Campbell is not the most exciting flight companion. She keeps falling asleep. But still, with her we are three and that is enough. And whenever we play astronauts, Michael Collins? We always, *always* survive the journey.

Along with the day I found out Buster wasn't mad at me after all for writing you and the day that I discovered how spectacular the library is, this is the best day so far this summer. Tomorrow is just drawing closer and closer, like a rocket zooming toward us, and it is all I can think about or Buster can talk about. When the clock said a few minutes after nine-thirty this morning, I thought he was going to die. "Holy moly! Less than twenty-four hours away now!" I think I was just as excited, but I was definitely quieter about it.

Then dinnertime came around, as it tends to do every day, and excitement about tomorrow was put into a holding pattern.

My mom had made spaghetti and meatballs, which is

normally one of my favorite things to eat. But not when it's so hot out. Buster says that for you astronauts, you'll still get to eat on your journey, but that the food is dried powder in a plastic bag that you mix with water from a water gun and then drink straight from the plastic bag. He says you can't have food in regular form because of the gravity situation on the ship, plus it's dangerous to your mission. The food could just float anywhere, and what would happen if you got green peas in your controls? So you have to survive on liquefied food from tomorrow until your return. I don't think I'd mind it so much with soup, but I'm not sure about drinking liquefied spaghetti and meatballs.

Buster also says that I don't want to know about what you three are going to have to do about going to the bathroom while in space, and I'll tell you something: Buster is right. I most definitely do not want to know that.

Anyway, there I was, sweating over my spaghetti and meatballs. And there my mom was, looking cool in her plaid Bermuda shorts, sleeveless top, and pearls—no matter how hot the weather, she always manages to look cool, which is one of life's mysteries. And there my dad was, still in his work clothes, which consist of navy-blue pants and a navy-blue button-down shirt with a white T-shirt underneath and boots and a belt, but with clean hands, since he always washes his hands first thing when he comes in the door. And there was Bess, though in body only, not in spirit. If Bess had her way, she'd be with Vinny every second of the day and evening, but Dad draws the line at dinnertime on weeknights. He says a family that doesn't eat together is like no kind of family at all. I think that's what he took the hardest about Eleanor moving out: not being able to see her face at the dinner table every night. Even though my mom stood up to my dad when Eleanor wanted to move out, I know my mom misses having Eleanor at the table, too, since Eleanor is the one most like my mom.

Perhaps the reason my mom looked so cool was because, unlike me, she didn't have the heat from the spaghetti and meatballs steaming up into her face. And that is because she'd pushed her plate away, her food uneaten. In its stead, she had a notepad and pencil, and she was making a list.

My dad ate in silence, using a big spoon to twirl his spaghetti against with the fork like he does, but he kept looking over at her with curiosity. Who could blame him? I wanted to know what was on that list, too. But he wasn't going to ask her, and if he wasn't, then I couldn't either. I'd just have to hope she'd tell us in good time. And that whatever was on the list, it would be something happy and not something that would become grounds for another "discussion."

"Okay," she finally said, as though she'd been in the midst of a conversation with someone. "I've got red with the Jell-O and white with the deviled eggs." She tapped her pencil against her lower lip. "But what am I going to do for blue?" She turned to me. "Mamie, can you think of any blue foods?"

"You could dye frosting blue like you did for the Fourth of July," I said, starting to feel excited, hoping this was going where I thought it might be going. "Or even a whole cake. Come to think of it, I'll bet you could dye almost anything blue."

"True. But I was hoping for something different, more natural. I was hoping not to have to dye anything."

"Jell-O's not naturally red," my dad spoke up.

"Excuse me?" she said.

"Read the box. It's got dye in it."

"I suppose you must be right. Of course it does. Oh, well." She shrugged. "Dyed frosting it is. Okay, I was also thinking cocktail franks for hors d'oeuvres and maybe, for the punch, I'd start with a base of Tang?"

"*Tang?*" my dad said.

"Have you ever tried Tang?" I asked her.

"No," she said, looking more interested in me than she had the past few days. "Why, have you?"

"Uh-huh. At Buster's request, Buster's mom's been buying it for us instead of Hi-C."

"And?"

"I'm getting used to it. But let's just say it's very tangy." I considered for a bit. "I suppose, if you added other things to it, though—perhaps some vanilla ice cream, in which case it might taste like a cough-medicine Creamsicle—and didn't rely on it for the whole of the punch, you might end up with something okay."

"I'll keep that in mind. Thanks, Mamie."

I felt proud I could help her out like that, but the good feeling didn't last for long because, apparently, my dad had had enough.

"Marlene," he said to her, "do you want to tell me just what the blazes is going on here?"

She didn't bother to answer. Instead, she tapped her pencil against her lip some more. "Whom to invite? Of course, Eleanor will come home for this. But who else?"

I hoped that, whatever she was planning, she'd include Buster's family. But I knew she wouldn't. We're just not those kinds of neighbors. Or at least Buster's parents and my parents aren't.

"The Carlsons?" she suggested, more to herself than anyone else. "The McGuires? Maybe the—"

"I thought I said no Launch Party," my dad said, cutting her off.

"You did, Frank," she said calmly, meeting his eyes for the first time, "and I heard you, loud and clear. There will be no Launch Party in this house."

"Good," he said with a grim nod.

"I realized you were right," she said.

"I was?" he said.

"Of course. Aren't you always? And how silly of me. Why, the astronauts are lifting off tomorrow morning and it's a weekday. I don't suppose you're going to take the day off to watch with us? Or at least the morning?"

"Of course not. I have to work. I can't be taking time off for this nonsense the whole country's gone crazy over."

"Right. You never take time off for any nonsense, do you, Frank?"

"No point in being lazy or crazy."

"Exactly. As soon as I realized you wouldn't be here to watch with us tomorrow, I saw how silly I was being. We can't throw a party if you're not even here."

"Then what's all this?" He waved a hand at her notepad and her pencil and her in general. "You're obviously planning a party, one I've been told nothing about, a party that somehow requires red and white and blue food items. Now, what I would like to know is: What sort of party might that be?"

It's not so hard keeping something to yourself when no one's asking you questions, but when someone does? And it's the right question?

Now that he'd asked it, it was like a light going on and a dam opening, all at once. Unable to contain her excitement, my mom reached across the table and covered my dad's hand with hers.

"A Moonwalk Party, Frank! Think about it! In just a few days, men will be walking on the moon. And what better way to enjoy it than with our family, with our friends. We could all gather around the TV and have great food and drinks and—"

"No." He removed his hand from hers.

Yet she just kept going when even I could have told her it was no use.

"But, Frank," she said, "it'll be the weekend! It's not like you'd have to take time off from work, like you would tomorrow. You won't be working at all. It'll even be at night!"

"Did you hear me, Marlene? I said no. Just because the whole country's gone crazy, it doesn't mean I have to be a part of it. I will not have it. Not in my house."

"It's my house, too, Frank," she said. "Shouldn't that count for something?"

"It does, of course it does, but—"

"Do you know something?" She didn't wait for an answer. "For once, maybe for the first time ever, the entire country is excited about the same thing."

"Not the entire country. Howard at work—"

"Fine, there are two of you who aren't excited."

"There are more people who think like me than you realize, Marlene."

"Terrific. You can all get together and have a grump party, then. Honestly, you're worse than the Grinch at Christmas. But think about this." She paused.

"I'm waiting," he said. "I can't start thinking about it until you tell me what it is."

"Tomorrow's going to come, Frank. Whether you like it or not, it's going to come. Tomorrow morning, three men are going to leave this planet and try to do something no one has ever done before. Who knows? Maybe you're right, Frank. Maybe the space race is dumb and it doesn't matter who wins it. Maybe this is all just a big waste of taxpayer dollars. But so what? Since it's going to happen anyway, why not enjoy it? Why not be excited? Whatever else happens in our lives, this will never happen again, not like this."

I couldn't tell what was going on in my dad's brain because his brain is his and mine is mine, but I knew what I was thinking—and that was: *I'm impressed.* I'd had no idea my mom could talk like that. If it were up to me and I was my dad, I'd just throw up my hands and say, "Lady, you win." Here was the part that was a little scary, though. Unlike other times when they'd had discussions, my mom's voice hadn't risen at all, not once. It hadn't even risen in the parts where the words were so emotional, it was impossible to figure out how a person's voice couldn't rise just then. Instead, from the moment she'd said, "It's my house, too, Frank," every single word had been flat.

I know in an earlier letter, I talked about how a voice can get flat sometimes when there's too much emotion, but this was the opposite of that. Her flat voice had no emotion at all.

"I'm thinking about what you said." My dad tilted his head to one side. "And now I'm done thinking about it." He straightened his head, picked up his fork. "No party."

I thought she'd yell at him then. I thought for sure she would. I wanted to yell at him myself, even though I never had before.

Instead, she quietly rose from her seat at the table.

"You know what your problem is, Frank?" she asked.

He looked up at her, swallowed a bite of spaghetti. "No. But I'm sure you're about to tell me."

"You have no romance in you, Frank, never have. Not even one single drop."

Then she walked away from the table, walked clear out of the room.

I heard the scrape of the hall closet door, the click of a clasp, the jangle of keys, and the click of a clasp again.

Then, as my father paid close attention to his food, my mother walked back in. Over her forearm she had the straw handbag she likes to use in the summer, the one that's like a small rectangular suitcase with the brown leather handle, and in her hand she had her car keys. Without a word to anyone, she walked to the door and straight out.

At the sound of the screen door slapping shut, my dad looked up. And at the sound of the car engine, I grew anxious. Even Bess looked, at least briefly, like she might be thinking about something other than Vinny.

"Dad?" I said, that anxious feeling only growing stronger as I spoke. My stomach hurt, and not from trying to eat spaghetti and meatballs on a hot summer night. "Aren't you going to go after her?"

"Nah." He took a bite of spaghetti. "Your mother just needs to blow off some steam. She'll be back."

Sincerely yours,
Mamie

Dear Michael Collins,

I thought I was done writing you for the day. I was so sure of that fact that I sealed up the last letter and put a stamp on it. Stamps are expensive, as you may know. Still, I am sending you an additional letter written on the same day because there is so much more to say.

As I write this letter, it is late at night and the house is quiet. Too quiet.

As soon as dinner was over, Vinny came by to pick up Bess. He tooted the horn, and out she went.

"It's like they have it timed to a science," my dad said.

And then it was just him and me. That's never happened before. Or if it has, I don't remember it.

"Aren't you going to go play outside with Buster?" he asked.

"I don't think so," I said. "Maybe not tonight."

"You sick?"

"No."

"Well, suit yourself."

When the phone rang almost right after that, he jumped for it.

"Marlene?" he said. Then: "Oh." He handed the phone to me. "It's for you. It's Buster."

"Hello?" I said.

"How come you didn't come over right after dinner to get me?" he asked.

"Something came up."

"Well, can you come now?"

I wanted to go. I did. But I looked over at my dad and it just didn't feel right. "Not tonight," I said.

"Don't you realize how few hours are left until lift-off? Soon it'll be twelve! And then eleven and—"

"I know, and I promise I'll watch it with you tomorrow. But tonight I'm going to stay in. There's, uh, some stuff I have to do for my parents."

"Okay, then."

"Okay, then."

I hung up the phone.

I caught my dad looking at me. I don't know if "relief" is the right word for what I saw on his face, but it was something.

"How about some television?" he suggested.

Considering how upset he'd been when my mother

bought it, I'd seen that he had already come to love that color TV in the short time we'd had it. Well, who could blame him?

"Shouldn't we do the dinner dishes first?" I said.

"Oh. Right. I suppose we should."

But when we got to the sink, he didn't appear to know what to do. This is something I'd noticed about him before: that he didn't seem to have much awareness of the things my mother did around the house or how she did those things. Even something like doing the dishes—it was a mystery to him. I'd actually never done the dinner dishes by myself before, but I'd certainly seen my mom do them enough times and sometimes she even let me help. So I showed my dad how to fill the sink with hot water, how to squirt the Palmolive in while the water ran. When I offered him rubber gloves, he held out his worker's hands.

"There's no saving these now," he said. "You use those, sweet pea."

When we'd dried the last dish, he turned to me and smiled. "TV time now?"

I smiled back.

He turned the TV on and right away he could see that on every channel, they were talking about the moon launch tomorrow. I would've liked to hear what they had to say, but as soon as he realized that's all there was, he snapped the set right back off.

"Reading, maybe?" he suggested.

I nodded. Then he grabbed his book and lay down on the couch going one way like he always does, but there was no mom there to go the other way and no Bess to sit in a chair, slouched down, leg dangling over one side. So while I lay on the floor on my stomach, in my usual position, it wasn't the same. The book I was reading was *Sounder*, by Mr. William H. Armstrong. I do not believe he is any relation to your commander on Apollo 11. But even though it is a very good book, I could not concentrate.

For the longest time I watched my dad slowly turning the pages of his book. Something felt off. Usually when he did this, I could see the attention in his eyes. And yet now it seemed to me that he was doing what I used to do back when I was a cheat-reader: just turning the pages for show without really seeing what was in front of him.

My dad was so sure that my mom would be back. I know this, because he said it many times while we both sat there, each of us pretending to read. "Your mother will be back soon."

Only she wasn't. At every sound, he'd look up, and so would I, only to realize it was just the house creaking.

The marble clock over the mantel ticked loud. The shadows across the room grew long. And still she didn't come.

"Wow," my dad said when the time had gone past ten, my bedtime this summer. "I guess she had a little more steam to blow off than I imagined. Still, she'll be back." He shrugged, but I wasn't quite sure I believed in that shrug. "Probably as soon as you fall asleep, she'll come walking right in."

Whether I believed his shrug or not, I liked the idea of that last part. At the very least, it gave me something to hope for.

"Why don't you go brush your teeth?" he said.

"Okay."

"And then, I don't know, what does your mother usually do next—tuck you in?"

"Yes, but you don't have to do that."

"I will, though. Just because your mom's not here at the moment, doesn't mean you deserve to get short-changed in the tucking-in department."

It was a nice idea, but as I saw when he came upstairs to do it a few minutes later, he was clearly in over his head.

"Blanket?" he asked.

"No, it's summer."

"Just the sheet, then?"

"Just the sheet."

"And then, what? It's been a long time since I did this."

"You used to do this?"

"When you were a baby. I don't expect you'd remember that."

I didn't, but I wished I did.

"Okay," I said. "Next I say my prayers."

"Out loud?"

Here's the thing, Michael Collins. I actually wanted to say them out loud. I thought it might be, you know, comforting—to hear the words out in the air. But I'd long since added you to the list of names of people I pray for every night, and I didn't want my dad to hear that. He was being so nice, even if he had no idea what he was doing. With my mom gone, I didn't want to set him off again.

"No," I said, "just to myself."

I closed my eyes then and prayed for everyone I loved and for you, too, Michael Collins.

When I opened my eyes, my dad leaned down and kissed me on the forehead. At least he got that part right.

"Good night," he said. "Sweet dreams. I'm sure your mom will be back by the time you get up in the morning."

Then he left, closing the door.

And now it's late at night. I haven't heard Bess come home yet. I haven't heard my mom come home. I haven't heard my dad come upstairs. Campbell is by my side as I write this. There is so much for me to worry about now, even more than I imagined when I got up this morning.

Can you sleep, Michael Collins? Because I can't.

Are you scared? Or just excited?

Good thing you're not reading this right now, because if you were, then you would know that I am terrified, about so many things.

Good night, Michael Collins. I hope tomorrow is everything you ever dreamed it would be.

Sincerely yours,
Mamie

Dear Michael Collins,

Today was every bit of what Buster said it would be and yet so, *so* much more.

Before we get to that part, though, I need to tell you what happened first, almost none of which is what a person might call good.

I must have finally fallen asleep last night because I woke up with my face smushed up against my last letter to you. Right away, I got up and put it in an envelope and then put a stamp on it for mailing later. When you get it, I hope you won't mind how crumpled the pages are.

While brushing my teeth, I tried to convince myself that the night before had been a bad dream and that my mom hadn't really left. Then I remembered what day it was, the launch finally here, so I picked out blue shorts and a red shirt and I even put a white headband on. I was trying to get the headband just right in the mirror—you are lucky you don't have to bother with women's accessories,

Michael Collins, because if you did you would know how hard it is to get a headband straight and how sometimes it just makes your hair clump funny—when I heard someone walking around in the kitchen. I stopped worrying about my hair and raced down there, figuring my dad had been right and my mom returned last night while I was sleeping.

But when I got to the kitchen, I skidded to a stop when I saw my dad. He had on his navy-blue work clothes—only from how rumpled they looked I guessed they were the same ones from the day before—and his eyes didn't look like he'd slept any.

"How come you're not at work?" I said.

"I thought I'd go in a little later today," he said. "I didn't want you to come down for breakfast and have no one be here."

That told me all I needed to know. My mom hadn't come back.

"Didn't Bess come home last night?" I asked.

"Oh, she's here. But you know your sister. Nothing short of a bomb can wake her before noon."

That was certainly true.

"Sit," he said, pointing at the table. "Now, then. What does your mom usually give you for breakfast?"

I thought about this. "Do we have any Froot Loops in the cabinet?" I asked hopefully.

I figured this wasn't a lie, because it's not like I was answering his question with that. I was simply asking another question. He could draw his own conclusions.

He looked through the cereal cabinet, found the box at the back that my mom reserved for special occasions. Placing a full bowl in front of me, he went to the fridge and got out the milk. Holding it over the bowl, he started to ask, "How much do you—"

"I can do it," I said, taking the container from him. I was thinking how odd it was, having him do these things for me, and thinking how good it would be if only my mom was there, too. But she wasn't. And I tell you, even looking at that bowlful of rainbow didn't help one bit, even with all the sugar I knew was coming with it, because it just made me sad. It turns out that there's some sad that even Froot Loops can't fix.

"Aren't you going to eat?" my dad said.

That didn't sound like it left me much choice, so I picked up my spoon. Then my dad poured himself a cup of coffee and sat down across from me. This should have felt like a prize, but it didn't. I just ate my cereal and he just stared into his cup until the phone rang, making us both jump. My dad lunged for it on the wall so fast, the table shook.

"Marlene?" he said, snatching it up. "Oh." He held out the phone to me.

"Buster?" I said.

My dad nodded. "Who else?"

I thought Buster deserved better than a disgruntled "Who else?" like he was some kind of annoyance. And yet I could see where my dad had a point. It wasn't Buster's fault, but it would have been nice if he were my mom right then.

"Hello?" I said. Then I listened to what Buster had to say, which was so full of excitement and "Holy moly!" it was hard not to get swept along with him. "Okay. I can ask."

I put my hand over the receiver. "Buster wants to know if he can come watch the launch over here. On the big TV."

I waited while my dad considered this. "I understand this is something that a lot of families are doing together," he said carefully. "Doesn't Buster's mom want him to stay there with her?"

That was a funny thing about my dad. So much of the time, it seemed like he had no idea what other people wanted. Certainly, he hadn't understood what my mom wanted with the Moonwalk Party, that it mattered to her and so maybe he should just go along with her on it because of that simple fact: because it was important to her. And yet here he was, worrying about Buster's mom's feelings.

"I'll ask," I said.

"Because you can always go to his house," my dad said.

Usually Buster's mom doesn't like us around on Wednesdays when she's cleaning, but I doubted very much she would be treating today like a regular Wednesday.

"Okay." I uncovered the receiver and relayed my dad's question. "Uh-huh," I said. "Uh-huh," I said again. Buster was so excited, he was giving me more information than was called for under the circumstances. "Uh-huh, I'll tell him."

I turned back to my dad, cutting all Buster had said down to a few sentences: "Buster says his mom doesn't mind. Says she's already got a house full of her lady friends there. Says he *really* wants to watch it on the big, new color TV with me."

"All right, then." My dad sighed. "I guess I can't fight it."

"He says okay," I said to Buster, knowing how excited

that would make him. Then I hung up before either Buster started saying too much again or my dad could change his mind.

I took my breakfast things to the sink, and almost immediately the phone rang again.

This time, my dad didn't lunge for it. This time, the phone having betrayed him twice before—once last night and once this morning—by it not being my mom, he'd already given up on it being the answer to his prayers.

"It's probably Buster again, with one more important thing to tell you that can't wait until he sees you in five minutes." He sighed, indicated the bowl and spoon in the sink with his chin. "I'll handle this."

I hurried to the phone. "Buster?" I said into it.

But it wasn't Buster.

"Mamie, is that you?" my mom's voice said.

"Yes," I said, feeling more relieved than I can say to hear her voice. And yet, somehow, cautious.

"Is your father there?" she said.

I looked back to see my dad filling the whole sink with soapy water like I'd shown him how to do with the dishes last night. I guess he didn't realize you didn't need to do all that for just one bowl, one spoon, and one cup.

"Yes," I said, feeling more cautious yet.

"Well, don't tell him it's me. I just didn't want you to worry."

"Where are you?"

"I'm at your aunt Jenny's." Aunt Jenny's her sister. "But there's no need for anyone else to know that just now."

"When are you coming back?" I asked.

"I'm . . . not."

WHAT? I wanted to scream that at her so bad. But I didn't say anything at all, because if I opened my mouth that scream would come out and even if my dad couldn't hear my whispers over the running water, he'd sure hear that.

"I'll try to call again," she said. "But Aunt Jenny's number is with the emergency numbers taped to the side of the phone. So you can reach me if you need me."

IF? I wanted to scream that, too. I wanted to scream *I need you now!* But the words wouldn't come and, like I already said, I didn't want to be too loud.

"I love you, Mamie," she said.

"I love you, too," I said, finally able to get some words out because I wanted her to hear that part. But it was no good. As soon as I finished saying the words, I could tell that the other end of the line had already gone dead.

The water had stopped running.

"You love Buster?" my dad said, smiling for the first time in quite a while. "Is that something you kids say to each other these days, like 'Peace'?"

"No," I said quietly. "Mom. I love Mom."

His smile went away so quickly, it was like it had never been there at all. Then he moved toward me fast, his face so serious and his hands grabbing on to both my arms so tight. It didn't hurt. My dad had never hurt me—never had, never would—but it was still scary.

"Why didn't you tell me?" he said.

"I didn't have time. She just said a few things and then she hung up."

"But she's okay?" he asked urgently.

I thought about this. How could she possibly be okay if she wasn't here with us?

And yet she'd sounded . . .

"Fine," I said. "She was fine."

He closed his eyes, his grip on me loosening a bit. "Thank God." Then his eyes shot open, that grip tightening right back up again. "Where is she?"

I tried to think of what she'd said exactly. "She says no one needs to know that right now."

"*Where is she?*"

I tell you, Michael Collins, I didn't want to betray her. But this wasn't like when my dad asked me what I usually have for breakfast. This wasn't just a question I could somehow turn away the truth with by using another question. And I couldn't lie to him.

"Aunt Jenny's," I said.

"Aunt Jenny lives two states away!" He let go of me. "Where's Aunt Jenny's phone number?"

"Taped to the side of the phone, but—"

He was already dialing.

"Put her on," he said to the voice at the other end of the line when someone answered. "I want to talk to my wife . . . I don't care if she doesn't want to talk to me. She's still my— Then I'll come down there to get her . . . Well, I *know* she's got her own car and that she could drive herself home if that was what she wanted. I just— Fine. If that's the way she wants it? *Fine.*"

He slammed the phone back on the hook.

And that was it.

My parents have been married for nearly twenty-five years—nearly a quarter of a century, they like to call it— so you'd think there would've been more, but there simply wasn't.

"She'll come around," my dad said, like he was

trying to convince someone of something. "I'm glad she's okay."

"Me too," I said.

And I was. I certainly didn't want anything bad to happen to her, not ever. But she'd said she wasn't coming back. I hadn't told him that part. He hadn't known to ask the question and, not being asked directly, I wasn't about to volunteer the information. I didn't want to believe it was true. I wanted to believe he was right, that she would be back. But what if my dad was wrong? What if she never came around?

My dad probably thought it was about the Launch Party and then the Moonwalk Party he'd said no to. He probably thought it had to do with what she said before she walked out, about him not having any romance in him. But for her not to stay, not to stay to at least fight about it some more, I knew it had to be more than just that, big as I could see those things were to her.

Before we could say anything else, there was a knock at the back door, followed by a whole series of rapid little knocks.

"Hold your horses," my dad said. "I'm coming, I'm coming."

I was right behind him, so I was there when he opened the door on Buster, who had a large glass pitcher in his hands, filled with orange liquid.

"Hello, Buster," my dad said.

"You stayed home for the launch, sir!" Buster said.

"Not exactly," my dad said. "But I suppose it's turning out that way."

"That's great, sir!" Buster said. "My dad went to work in the city. But he said they'll all go over to the appliance store across the street and watch it on the TVs there, so that's all right, I guess. Oh, and look!" He started waving the pitcher around. "I brought Tang!"

My dad quickly relieved Buster of the pitcher before Buster could slosh the contents all over the kitchen floor, which looked close to happening.

"That's mighty thoughtful of you, Buster," he said.

"I think there's enough for everyone!" Buster said.

"Well, that's just great. Why don't you and Mamie . . . ?" He used his pitcher-free hand to indicate the direction of the living room, but it was a halfhearted gesture and mostly I just got the impression that he was ready to be rid of us.

With the distracting swerving pitcher out of the picture, I could now see that Buster's great mind had thought like mine. He had on navy shorts and a red shirt, but no white headband.

"You wore navy, too, today, sir!" Buster said, pleased. "In honor of the moon launch?"

"No, Buster," my dad said. "That's what you call a coincidence. These are just my regular work clothes."

"I have to say," Buster said, "it's probably a good thing your work clothes aren't all red. I suspect, if you don't mind me saying, that you'd look funny in all red."

"You're probably right about that, Buster."

As we started toward the living room, Buster turned back to my dad. "Aren't you going to come watch with us?"

"I don't think so," my dad said. "But wait."

He pulled two glasses from the cabinet and poured Tang for me and Buster, handing the glasses over. Then he seemed to consider something and pulled a third glass out, filling that one, too. He raised his glass in our direction. "Cheers." Then he took a glug that left him with a surprised look.

"Great, isn't it?" Buster said.

"Not quite the word I was looking for, Buster."

"I know," I told my dad, "but you get used to it, kind of."

Buster tugged on my hand.

In the living room, I suppose we could have sat on the couch to watch. No one else was using it. But we were so used to taking positions on the floor, because older people would claim the better seats, that we just plopped right down. Then I crawled forward on my knees to switch the TV set on.

And I'll tell you, when I turned that set on, it was like magic. Even with the excitement of Buster being at my house, even with the excitement of being allowed to drink something as colorful as Tang in the living room no matter what it actually tasted like, there'd still been a shadow over the day. How could I enjoy myself when my parents were fighting and my mother was gone and who knew what all else might happen? And yet, as soon as that color picture popped into my living room and I saw all those people waiting down in Florida for the launch of Apollo 11, everything bad fell away. It's not that I wasn't worried about my mom anymore, because deep down I was. But it's not like she'd left Earth. She was just somewhere that wasn't here. You, though—you were about to leave Earth. I couldn't even feel bad about that right then, not worried or scared like I'd been the night before, because it was all just too incredible.

There you were, walking out to the launch pad with Neil Armstrong and Buzz Aldrin, waving to the crowd.

It didn't even bother me when Buster said, "Hey, where's your mom? Isn't she going to watch this?" and all I could say was "No" and "I'll fill you in later."

"What about Bess?" he said. "Isn't she home?"

"Sleeping," I said. "Normally, she's not up for another three hours or more. You know that."

"Wake her," Buster said. "She'll be sorry forever if she misses this."

So I did, even though she yelled at me, even though I was worried I'd miss it myself because she was taking so long to get out of bed, I just kept tugging and tugging on her arm until finally she gave in and let me pull her downstairs. I rejoined Buster on the floor, with Bess behind us on the couch.

While I'd been gone, you must have gotten inside the *Columbia*, strapping yourselves in, doing final preparations. Buster had told me that the three of you astronauts would be seated on your backs, that that's how astronauts fly, on your backs, facing the sky, and I wondered what it must be like to be you right then, feeling what you were feeling, seeing what you were seeing.

There was just one tense moment for me.

"Takeoffs," Buster said. "In anything that flies, that's one of the most dangerous parts."

And then the countdown reached the final seconds— *TEN . . . NINE . . .* —and I couldn't help it because I really heard Buster when he'd said Bess would be sorry forever if she missed this—*FIVE . . . FOUR*—I yelled out, "Daddy! Come on! Daddy! Come here!"

And he did.

I heard his footfall entering the room right on *ONE*, felt him by my side as the Saturn V rocket powered you in Apollo 11 off the ground. Even on the TV, the sound it made going up was like a volcano erupting with white-hot flames and gas spewing from the engine nozzles. There was so much billowing smoke and fire, I couldn't help but think again how that did not look like a good idea, but then I forced myself to remember that you need that fire to get you where you want to be.

I heard a gasp and looked quickly at my dad—his mouth was hanging open, something like awe on his face. But then my eyes immediately went back to the screen as you rose higher and higher and higher. Buster cheered so loud then and I cheered with him and I swear we were so loud together they could have heard us down in Florida and some Tang sloshed out of Buster's glass and onto the carpet and my dad didn't even say one word about it.

And then we all just watched, watched you in your rocket trailing fire behind you until we couldn't see you anymore, and that's what I meant when I started this letter by saying "Today was every bit of what Buster said it would be and yet so, *so* much more," because it was and because even though I'm using words to write this letter, words truly cannot express what it was like to see you do that today.

I don't think my dad could express it either. When I first got up this morning, he'd said he was still going into work, only later. But after that, he couldn't bring himself to leave. Not then.

When we couldn't see you anymore, I was relieved, because I remembered what Buster had said about take-offs being one of the most dangerous parts of flying. At 9:32 a.m. today, Michael Collins, you left Earth. You survived takeoff. If Buster was right, as he is about most things, you started out with a million and one things that could go wrong with your mission. It may not seem like much, but one less thing to worry about is still one less thing to worry about, and today I will gladly take that.

The way I figure it, now there are just a million things left that could go wrong.

Sincerely yours,
Mamie

Thursday, July 17, 1969

Dear Michael Collins,

What did you see, lying there facing the sky? I wish I could have seen what you saw at liftoff. I wish you could have seen what I saw, what the world saw, from the ground. Maybe when you get back—I refuse to say "*if*"— somehow, you will see it. They keep on showing it again and again on TV. They'll probably keep showing it forever. But it's not the same. It's not like seeing it for the first time, when it was actually happening, the hope of success and the fear of disaster.

Buster says that even though the people on TV are still talking and talking about you, there really won't be anything new to see for a few more days, not until you get to the moon.

It's funny how, if you know someone well or think you do, even if they're not right in front of you and you can't really see them, in your mind you still think you can.

I picture my mom two states over with Aunt Jenny,

watching the same things we are seeing on the TV here about you and your flight.

I picture you in the *Columbia*, floating around inside now, eating dried foods made liquid by firing water from a gun into bags.

As you may have guessed, yesterday evening, for the second night in a row, my mother did not come home.

Yesterday, after all there was to see had ended and my dad left the room and Bess went back upstairs to bed, I told Buster that my mom had gone to stay with my aunt for a bit. If he thought it was strange, her leaving at a time like this and with me not having said anything about her going away beforehand, he didn't let on. But then today, something happened that put that right out the window, which I will get to in a moment.

It turns out my dad knows as much about cooking as he does about doing the dishes. By this I mean when it came time for dinner last night, he went to the store and came back with TV dinners, which is something my mother never buys. In fact, I had never had one before and it was quite a treat, seeing my meal all laid out in four nifty little compartments: the Salisbury steak, the mashed potatoes, the green beans, and the apple crisp. Bess, being perhaps less enthusiastic than I was at the prospect of a TV dinner, asked if she could go out with Vinny instead and, I guess since Mom is gone, Dad figured that family dinners weren't so important anymore and he just let her go without a fight. We don't own TV trays, which might have been fun, so instead we made do with the coffee table in the living room, and that felt like it might almost be as much fun. It would've been better if my mom were there, too, though, even if TV dinners are not something that she would ever, *ever* buy.

Once again, I did not go to Buster's after dinner. Once again, I told Buster there was stuff I needed to do for my parents.

I suppose my dad must've been thinking the same thing, that it would've been better if my mom could be there, too: thinking it throughout the night as we watched TV together and then read, thinking it as he tucked me in, thinking it as he lay in bed alone. Because this morning when I came down to breakfast, there was a different energy in the air. My dad was sitting at the kitchen table and there was a bowl already filled with Froot Loops, without me even having to ask for them. I felt that new energy crackling off him as I tried to eat my bowlful of rainbow, which already tasted better than it had the day before.

And then somewhere between my finishing half and three-quarters of my cereal, my dad abruptly got up from the table.

"I can't stand it anymore," he said.

I did want to know what he meant by that, but I didn't think it a good idea to follow him as he stomped upstairs. I figured it would probably be best to just stay and eat my cereal. Whatever he was thinking about, whatever he was planning as I heard thumps and drawers opening and the shower running and other activity, soon enough I'd know.

Were you aware that if you watch two individual pieces of Froot Loops in a bowl of milk and they are each a different color, you can see the dye coming off them, making a new color in the milk between the two that is a little bit like each one? It is a fact, Michael Collins. I suspect NASA will have you doing more important experiments than this in space, but trust me, in case you never get to try this one out for yourself, it is a fact.

When my dad came downstairs, he was wearing fresh clothes for the first time in two days, his hair was damp, and in one hand he had a suitcase. It was the battered brown leather one that's always his when we go to Lake

George every other year. My mom says he's had it since their honeymoon and that it is an embarrassment, but he will never let her buy him a new one.

"Are we going somewhere?" I asked.

A part of me started to get excited. Were we going on a trip? We hardly go anywhere. But a part of me just wanted to stay put, what with everything going on in the world and space and all. Even if I can't see you anymore, at least at home I can turn on the TV and see simulations or have reporters tell me where the scientists say you must be in your flight right now or what NASA says you all are doing.

I needn't have worried, though. Or at least, not about that.

"Not we," my dad said. "Me."

"Where are you going?" I asked, rising out of my chair as I started to feel a touch of panic. It would be fine for him to go outside to check if it's going to be another scorcher. Or go to the A&P for more TV dinners. Or go back to work. I'd even welcome that. But going somewhere dressed in casual clothes and trailing a suitcase? And without me? "Where are you going?" I asked more urgently when he didn't answer at first because he was too busy counting the money in his wallet.

"I'm going to see your mom," he said.

"But she doesn't want you there," I said, the words flying out of my mouth before I could help myself or stop them. Still, it was only the truth. She'd said as much to me, and even though I'd only heard his side of the conversation he had with Aunt Jenny, I'd still been able to tell that she'd told him my mom didn't want to see him.

"So I'll stay at a motel," he said. "Eventually, she'll have to talk to me."

I wasn't sure that was the case. From the tone in her voice when I'd spoken with her, I didn't think she felt like she ever had to talk to him again.

"But what about me?" I said. Because, selfish as it sounds, that really was the big thing. My mom was already gone. Who knew when, if ever, she'd be back? Having lost one parent already, I couldn't lose the other one. Okay, so maybe he isn't much of a parent in a lot of regards. He needed to be told how to do the dishes. He didn't know how to tuck me in. He bought TV dinners— well, that part wasn't so bad. But at least he is something and he has been learning real quick. I just couldn't lose him, too. Without the two of them, what would I have left?

"You'll stay here," he said, "with Bess."

"*Bess?*" I couldn't keep the scorn out of my voice, and I know he must have heard it there. But surely, even he knew: Bess was no solution to anything.

"She is sixteen," he said.

"With both cars gone," I pointed out, "it's not like she can take me anywhere if there's an emergency."

"What kind of emergency?" For the first time, he seemed to consider this possibility.

"How should I know?" I threw up my hands. "Stuff does happen!"

"Then call Eleanor. As a matter of fact, call Eleanor anyway after I leave. Have her come and stay with you."

"Eleanor can't come. She won't. Eleanor has a job."

"Eleanor is a secretary. It's not like the world is going to stop spinning if she comes in late every now and then or even misses a whole day."

I wasn't sure Eleanor would agree with his assessment of her importance, or lack of importance, but even I could see that she might be the only game in town.

"Could you call her for me?" I asked.

"I don't have time for that right now, sweet pea. I need to get on the road. I just want to get to your mother."

"But what about food? What if Eleanor can't come right away?"

"Good point," he said. He handed me some bills. "I'll go to the bank on my way out of town."

As much as I'd tried to stop it, this was really happening. And now, having made up his mind, I could see by the way he picked up his suitcase abruptly, he was clearly itching to be gone.

"How long will you be?" I said, hurrying after him as he strode toward the door, making me feel like the little dog scampering around the big dog like you see in all those cartoons. He went right out the door and I followed after, still the little dog.

"I don't know, sweet pea," he said, stopping just long enough to turn and kiss me on the forehead before spinning away once again. "Be good for your sisters!" he called over his shoulder before climbing into the car.

"Will you call at least?" I shouted.

But it was too late.

The car door was shut, the ignition had been turned on, and then he really was gone.

I waved at the disappearing car. Then I looked down at the money in my hands. Forty dollars. It was more money than I'd ever held in my life. But how long would it last me? How long would it need to?

I hurried inside and shut the door, ashamed of myself for shouting in the driveway and giving the neighborhood reason to talk about us.

Then, thinking about what my dad had said, I looked for Eleanor's number taped to the side of the phone and dialed it.

"Mamie!" she said, sounding surprised to hear from me. "You just caught me heading out the door on my way to work! What's up?"

I told her about Mom leaving two nights ago.

She wasn't surprised at that. "About time," she said.

I told her about Dad leaving to go after Mom. She was back to being surprised. "I never would've guessed he had it in him," she said. "But who's staying with you?"

I told her Bess was. Then I told her what Dad said, about the world still spinning if she was late to work or even missed a day—and here I added "or more."

That's when she said, "Isn't that just like him?" Sometimes people say that about another person with affection in their voice—I know, because I've heard it said that way, and I've even thought it before about

Buster—but this wasn't one of those times. "Tell you what," she added. "You should be fine with Bess today. Do you have enough food?"

I put down the phone long enough to check the cabinets and the freezer. I still had Froot Loops. And I usually had lunch at Buster's house.

"Uh-huh," I told her, once I'd picked up the phone again.

"Great," she said. "Tomorrow's Friday. I can come by then. Fridays aren't so busy at work in the summer. And with the moon launch and everything, no one's doing much work anyway. So I'll see you tomorrow. Bess can't do too much damage in one day. Be good, squirt!"

And then she was gone, too, before I could say anything else or even thank her.

So I went upstairs to Bess's room. For the second day running, I shook her awake before her usual time.

"What is it?" she said, groggy, staring with one eye shut at her alarm clock. "Are men leaving for the moon again?"

I told her about Dad leaving, to go after Mom.

"You woke me up for that?" she groaned.

"He said for you to watch me," I told her.

"Well," she said, "what do you usually do this time of day?"

Of course she wouldn't know. She was always sleeping this time of day.

"I usually go over Buster's house," I told her.

"Then do that." She pulled the pillow over her head to let me know she was done with me.

So that's what I did. I went to Buster's house.

But first I stopped at the phone in the kitchen. I thought I should call my mom, tell her what was going on here. She'd said I could call her at Aunt Jenny's anytime. But if I told her my dad was on his way to her, maybe she'd take off? I didn't want that.

Before leaving the house, I took the phone off the hook. I knew what would happen then. I'd hear the dial tone; then after that went on for a bit, it would be replaced by a string of loud beeps, after which: silence, even though the person calling would still get a busy signal.

It's not that I wanted my mom to get a busy signal if she called, far from it. But my parents always say that when no one is going to be home, you should leave the phone off the hook so if people call they'll think someone is home tying up the line. My parents say if you don't do this, if some bad person calls and no one answers, they may decide that since no one is home, it's okay to come to your house and steal all your stuff. My parents always take the phone off the hook when no one will be home, whether we're going to Lake George for a whole week or if my mom's just running out to the grocery store for a few items, because you can never be too careful.

Of course, Bess was home. But everyone knows Bess won't get up to answer a ringing phone until at least noon.

When I got to Buster's house, Mrs. Whitaker let me in and, I must say, it was satisfying, how excited she was to talk to me about the moon launch yesterday. At my own house, you'd think that nothing extraordinary had happened at all. Well, except for both my folks leaving.

"Isn't it amazing, Mamie," she said, "to think that right now, those brave astronauts are rocketing toward the moon?"

I allowed that this was true, and I meant every single word of it.

"I suppose you're here to see Buster," she finally said.

I allowed how that was true, too, and she pointed me toward the basement.

What a strange day this was turning out to be. Already, I'd had more conversations with different people and for longer than I ever usually did on any given summer day.

Once I was with Buster, though, it was odd. It was odd because in just one short spin of the Earth, so much had changed for me. When you have a best friend, and perhaps you know this already, you have to tell him when something important happens in your world, like I should have told Buster from the beginning about how I was writing to you.

So I told him about how my mother left two days ago, only this time I finally told him why, and then I told him how my dad had now left, too.

"Wow, Mamie," he said. "Just wow!" Only he didn't add *"Holy moly!"* because I guess he knew this wasn't something I was excited about. "What are you going to do?"

I told him how my dad had said that it was okay, that I would be with Bess.

"Aw, Bess." He waved a hand. "Bess is no use."

And here is something else about best friends, Michael Collins, although maybe you already know this, too: They always know stuff like this. They always know what's what and what matters in your life.

"You know," he said, "if I tell my mom what's going on, I'm sure she'll say you can stay with us."

And just like that, relief at having shared my problem with a friend turned to sheer terror.

"Please don't do that!" I said.

"How come?" he said, puzzled.

But how could I explain? How could I explain that even now, with both parents gone, I felt like I wanted—no, needed—to stay in my own house?

"It'll be fine," I said, forcing a smile. "Eleanor's coming tomorrow."

"Oh!" he said, clearly relieved on my behalf. "Why didn't you say something before? If Eleanor's coming, then everything's fine!"

I wasn't about to tell him, not now, but everything felt far from fine.

"Then you won't tell your mom?" I said, still feeling anxious about it.

"Not if you don't want me to, I won't," he said, and he made the "Scout's honor" gesture, even though neither of us has ever been a Scout.

Then he asked if I wanted to play astronauts, and I

said I did, and he asked if I could go get Campbell to be Buzz, and I did, which was not easy because Campbell is just getting fatter and lazier by the day.

And so the three of us played at being you three astronauts, getting closer and closer to the moon.

Sincerely yours,
Mamie

Dear Michael Collins,

Last night, after a TV dinner, I tucked myself into bed. It was a little lonely, yet somehow I managed.

Bess was home, but she was on the phone with Vinny all night, which is as good as no one being here. Without parents around to stress to her the importance of family dinners, she didn't even bother to eat with me. I tried telling her to get off the phone in case one or both of our parents were trying to call, but she wouldn't listen.

Once I was there in bed, alone in the dark except for Campbell, for the first time all day I had a chance to think and then all sorts of thoughts began flooding in.

When my dad left and after I'd been upset in the driveway, I'd called Eleanor, woken up Bess, went to see Buster, came home, and did the things I had to do around the house, like taking care of myself and feeding Campbell and watering the tomatoes in the garden. Maybe another person would've panicked more or for longer, seeing her dad's taillights come on at the stop sign and then him pulling away. But what choice did I have? The grown-ups weren't acting like grown-ups—if you ask me, they were both acting like crazy little kids—and someone had to make sure things went on happening like they're supposed to around here.

Perhaps you understand what this is like, Michael Collins. Really, you of all people must know. An emergency happens—you have a fire on your F-86—what do you do? Do you start to panic? Break out into tears? No. Of course not. You react immediately. You start flipping the switches that need to be flipped, you follow proper procedure, you pull the cord on the parachute if you have to, you do whatever needs to be done, putting one foot in front of the other without taking time to actually think about the real emergency, because that's the one thing you don't have: time. So you go on autopilot because that is the only choice you have to survive. You understand that, right?

But then, once the immediate danger has passed, all the emotion comes.

And for me, lying there in bed, that's when I began thinking: What if my dad is wrong? He seems to think he can patch things up quickly, like putting a Band-Aid on a skinned knee. But what if he can't? And what if my mom isn't just mad for now but mad forever—is it really possible that she will never come back?

That's when a dreaded word entered my brain and that word is

Divorce.

Sure, I've heard of people getting divorced before. But those were always made-up characters like Michael and Claire on *As the World Turns.* Or celebrities, like last year, Frank Sinatra the singer got divorced from Mia Farrow the actress after just two years of marriage, which my parents said was no surprise, since their age difference was about the same as that between Delores Doyle's parents. Or like John Lennon from the Beatles getting divorced by his wife, Cynthia, last year, so now he's with Yoko Ono.

The girls at school are gaga over the Beatles, always talking about which one they like best, Paul or John. If I had to choose, I'd go for George Harrison. *Maybe* Ringo. But really, I prefer the Rolling Stones. Bess belongs to the Columbia Record Club, and albums come to the house every month, so I have had a lot of opportunity to compare the two.

But those people I mentioned? The ones who've

gotten divorced lately? All made-up people or celebrities. No one on my *street* has ever gotten divorced. No one's parents in my class at *school* have ever gotten divorced, not even Delores Doyle's.

Divorce.

Is such a thing possible?

Could it happen to my parents?

And if it did, what would happen to me?

That's what occupied my mind last night.

Today I couldn't play with Buster right away because Eleanor arrived bright and early, without even calling first, but that was okay. I was just plumb relieved. She didn't come in hauling a suitcase, but that was okay, too. I figured she had it in the trunk of her car.

I hadn't realized how completely alone I'd been feeling, even with Bess and Campbell asleep in the house, until I saw Eleanor come through the door.

Sometimes it amazes me how little I see of Bess, given we live under the same roof. My mom says having a teenager is like living with a ghost, one you never see unless she needs money. Of course, Eleanor hadn't been that way—at least, not according to my parents—but Bess certainly is. I wonder what I'll be like when I am a teenager.

"Where's Bess?" Eleanor asked right away.

I pointed toward the ceiling. "Still sleeping."

"About what I expected," she said. "So I'm here. What do you need me to do for you?"

I wanted to tell her that what I really needed right about now was a hug. But I didn't want her to think I was just some baby. So instead, I said, "I don't know." I thought about it. "Could you take me food shopping?"

"Let's see what you need . . ." She started going through cabinets, opening the freezer and fridge. The cereal boxes, when she shook them, were almost empty and I guess she wasn't impressed by that lone remaining TV dinner, because she said, "Looks like you need every-thing, squirt. Come on, then."

"Wait," I said.

"Why?"

"I need to call Buster and tell him I won't be avail-able to play this morning."

So that's what I did.

"Can you come later?" he asked when I told him.

"I'm not sure," I said. Then I explained how Eleanor had arrived. "So you really don't have to worry about things and me anymore," I said. "Everything's just fine now. I have adult supervision."

"The cavalry has arrived!" he shouted, laughing.

"Exactly," I said, laughing back.

After hanging up, I lifted the receiver off the hook and set it down.

"What are you doing?" Eleanor asked. Before I could explain about keeping the house safe from criminals, she reached out and ruffled my hair. "So responsible. Mom and Dad sure have you well trained. But Bess is home."

I gave the only response to that a person could, raising both eyebrows at her as high as they could go.

"You're right," she agreed, laughing. "Everyone knows Bess won't answer a phone before noon, and sometimes not even then."

I grabbed the money that my dad left me, and we went.

It was a good thing that Eleanor had kept the windows to her car open. You may not know this, spending most of your time in rocket ships and such, but if you get into a car in the summer without rolling down the windows first, it is like a bath of steam flowing out at you, and then when you close the door it is like an oven.

"You be thinking about what you want to get at the A&P," Eleanor said.

Right then it occurred to me that we should have made

a list first, like Mom always does, because as soon as she said that, I felt knocked over. I wasn't used to having it be up to me what to get at the supermarket and thinking ahead to all the choices made my head start to hurt, so instead I asked her about her work.

"I suppose Dad's right for once," she said. "It's not the most important job in the world, but at least it pays the rent."

"Do you like it?" I asked.

"Oh, it's all right," she said. "Some of the other secretaries, though, they can be a little mean."

"Well, do you have at least one friend there?" I asked.

She thought about this for a while. "Yeah," she said. "I guess I do."

"You're all right, then," I said. "You know, you only need the one."

She thought about this for a while, too. Finally, she said, "I suppose that's true," and then she smiled.

That made me feel good. It made me feel good that I had pointed out to her something about the way the world works that she may not have noticed before.

"If it's only all right, though," I asked, "don't you ever think about doing something else?"

"Sure," she said. "But when I first elected to go to

secretarial school, it seemed like a good idea. Most of my friends from high school got married right after graduation. And even the ones who didn't? The ones who went on to college? They were just doing it until they met the right guy. Me, I thought I was choosing a career. But it turns out that you're mostly just waiting on someone else. And now that I've moved out, I have bills to pay, and the choices don't seem so many."

"So what career would you have," I asked, "if you could switch?"

"Stewardess?" she said, like it was a question. But the way she answered so quickly, I knew she'd given this some thought.

"*Stewardess?*" I was surprised. "But isn't that just like waiting on other people all the time, too, only in a different way?"

"Well, yeah," she conceded. "But you also get to see the world. You get to fly."

It seems like everything these days is about leaving the ground and getting up in the air. Me, I've never been on a plane before. But I've seen ads for airlines in my mom's magazines—Eastern Air Lines, TWA, Pan Am— and sometimes, in addition to the planes, there are pictures of glamorous stewardesses in their uniforms. Those uniforms always look so neat and crisp, and the steward-esses always look so confident and excited, like they know they're going places.

"I guess that could be okay," I said.

"It could," Eleanor agreed.

"So why don't you still try?" I said. "To be a stewardess, I mean."

"Maybe," she said. "Maybe I still will."

"You know," I said, remembering something I'd read during my trip with Buster to the library, "Michael Collins, after seeing John Glenn on Mercury Atlas 6, deci-ded to become an astronaut, but he wasn't accepted right away, and yet he just kept trying until he was. So you see, sometimes these things just take time."

She seemed a little surprised at my speech. All she said was "Huh," but it was the kind of "Huh" that told me maybe I'd given her something else to think about that hadn't occurred to her before.

"Just ignore the others in the office," I advised, refer-ring to her problem with the other secretaries again, "and focus on the one."

After that, we drove the rest of the way to the A&P in silence, the breeze through the open windows ruffling our hair.

When we got to the A&P, my headache over all the choices returned. Of course, I'd been to the supermarket with Mom, more times than I can count, but it'd never been up to me to do the deciding.

"What do you want to get?" Eleanor asked, pushing the empty cart.

All those aisles, all those decisions—it was too much for me.

Eleanor must have seen some of what I was feeling in my face, because she said, "Why don't we start with the cereal?"

That was a relief. When we were in the cereal aisle, though, even that felt like too much. I couldn't pick between the *should* of Cap'n Crunch and the *want* of Froot Loops, so I finally wound up getting both.

"What else?" she said.

I couldn't think of anything so she said, "How about some more frozen dinners?" She sighed as she pushed the cart toward the frozen food aisle. "Those are easy and convenient."

She took a whole bunch of boxes from the freezer case, and it was a little thrilling, seeing the quantity of selections there.

And then I had an idea, and an even bigger thrill came into me, washing the headache away.

"Can I get some chicken?" I asked, excited.

"What?"

I didn't answer. I knew where the chicken was kept, in the poultry department, and I made straight for it, Eleanor trailing behind me with the cart.

"Mamie," she said as I tossed a package of chicken in the cart, "do you even know how to cook chicken?"

I ignored that question, too, instead tapping my finger against my lower lip, just like adults always do when they're thinking.

"Now, then," I said. "Where do they keep the soup . . . ?"

I found the Campbell's cream of mushroom soup and tossed in a can.

Then I remembered red Jell-O, followed by cocktail franks, and the white cake mix and white frosting mix. I even read the directions on the backs so I'd know what other ingredients I might need. I didn't think I needed any new blue dye, figuring that dye's not something you run out of real quick and that we probably still had some at home left over from the Fourth of July, and red from

Christmas, too—I was planning to do something special with my cake. I didn't know how long my dad's forty dollars needed to last me and, even giddy as I was feeling, I didn't want to waste any of that forty dollars that I didn't have to. Then I remembered potato chips and the fixings for dip, too, because you can't have a party without dip.

We circled the aisles of the supermarket so many times as I remembered different things that eventually Eleanor said, "Do you even know what you're doing, squirt?"

I did. Outside the frozen food case, I'd had a grand idea, which was this: My mom had wanted to have a Moonwalk Party on Sunday. My dad had said no. My mom left. My dad went after her. But you know what I realized? A Moonwalk Party is still a terrific idea. So I would throw one myself on Sunday, even if my parents weren't home. I'd make the special chicken and the other special foods, and we'd have our own Moonwalk Party, just me and Eleanor and Bess. If Bess insisted, Vinny could come. And Buster, he could definitely come, if his mom would let him. Plus Campbell—she'd be real happy about that chicken.

Just because my parents weren't there, it didn't mean that everything had to stop, and it was my responsibility to see to it that things kept going, like by having the Moonwalk Party we should have been having in the first place.

But I couldn't tell Eleanor this, not without ruining the surprise. So when she asked me her question—"Do you even know what you're doing, squirt?"—I just stared blankly back at her. I figured if I did that long enough, kind of like in a staring contest but being sure to look as dull and stubborn as I could, eventually she'd just get disgusted or bored, one or the other.

"Fine," Eleanor said, clearly giving up on me and my unusual food selections. "At least let's pick out something well rounded. What do you like to eat that I might be able to cook for you?"

What? Sure, she'd said she'd come over and then she'd said she'd take me shopping. But adults had let me down so much lately, I hadn't dared let myself hope for much beyond that. But now, not only had she come to stay with me, she was also going to cook something for me other than TV dinners? This was such a revelation, I just said in my excitement, "Anything. Anything at all that you would like to make for me, I am *sure* I would love to eat it."

I must say, I had not planned on that involving salad.

But you know what, Michael Collins?

The way she made it later on, it was good. At the A&P, she went back for another package of chicken. Then she added lettuce and a bunch of vegetables to the cart. I asked her not to forget the green goddess dressing, but she said she was going to get some other ingredients and just make her own dressing.

After we got home, we unloaded the bags of groceries from the car and I put the phone back on the hook. Then we put away the TV dinners in the freezer and the rest of the things I'd picked out. Right then and there, Eleanor roasted that chicken she'd bought. Afterward, she refrigerated it. Many hours later, she shredded it and spread the pieces over the top of the salad she prepared, and poured her own dressing over it. And let me tell you, salad with cold chicken on it makes for quite a refreshing meal in the summer.

We ate it in the dining room, like it was a special occasion, late in the afternoon, which seemed early to me for dinner, but I wasn't about to complain. We used the good dishes and silverware. Even Bess was there. I guess with Eleanor in the house, Bess felt bound by family dinners again. Or maybe she just liked having Eleanor around. It was a lively meal.

Mostly, the other two talked. Bess talked about

Vinny, and Eleanor talked about a new man she is dating. Talk of dating—I didn't really have anything to contribute to that. But still, I felt very grown-up and lively myself, just listening to the two of them.

At one point, Eleanor said again the thing she'd said to me on the phone the day before, about not being surprised that our mom had left, and Bess agreed with her.

"Why do you keep saying that?" I asked, starting to feel mad at them.

"Because it's true." Eleanor shrugged.

"They've always had discussions," I said. "I see no reason why it should be any different this time." I said that more because I wanted it to be true than because I actually believed there was any chance it was.

"I don't think she's ever been happy," Eleanor said.

"How can you say that?" I said.

"Because it's true," she said again with another shrug. "When she and Dad both dropped out of college to get married, she was pregnant with me . . ."

I must confess, Michael Collins, however Eleanor finished that sentence, whatever anyone else said for a while, I didn't hear it. I was too shocked.

It's a funny thing about parents. When they're your own, you tend to see them the way you've always seen them, meaning how you've known them in your lifetime and nothing else.

So, sure, I knew my parents had both been to college for a while and that neither had finished. But I'd never really thought much about what they were like before me. I certainly had never thought about what they were like before Eleanor. And I'd definitely never done the math and come up with them both leaving college early *because* of Eleanor.

I came back into the conversation on Bess saying, "I guess she always wanted more."

"What more?" I said.

"Just more," Eleanor said. "She wanted to finish college. She wanted to be more."

I thought about that, how after knowing my mom for ten years, I'd never seen that about her. But then, I started wondering about my dad, too. Maybe he'd wanted to finish college, too? Maybe, at one point, a part of him had wanted—and maybe still did want—more?

And yet he'd obviously never given Eleanor or Bess that impression, not like my mom had. As for me, all I could ever remember him saying was stuff like "A man's job is to take care of his family" or "A man's job is to put food on the table and a good roof over his family's heads."

But maybe he, too, would have wanted more if he had had a choice in the matter?

It was too much to think about at once, so I was grateful when Eleanor—elegant Eleanor!—let out a loud belch and we all just broke up laughing. In a tense moment, it is amazing how useful bodily functions can be as an icebreaker.

The three of us did the dishes together, laughing the whole time, with Campbell lazily weaving her way in and out among our feet. But the last dish was hardly dried and put away when there came a car horn, which is the telltale sound of Vinny.

"Where do you think you're going?" Eleanor called after Bess.

"Out," Bess said. "With Vinny."

"Not tonight you're not," Eleanor said.

"I'm not?" Bess said.

"How can you?" Eleanor said. "Who will stay here with Mamie?"

The panic I immediately felt took the good feelings I'd had since Eleanor arrived that morning and knocked them clear away.

"You're not staying?" I said to Eleanor. Suddenly I remembered something. Back at the A&P, when we went to put the grocery bags in the trunk, the trunk had been empty. I guess I'd been so excited at all the things we bought, and at the idea of the Moonwalk Party, I hadn't noticed enough at the time to think about what it might mean, that Eleanor didn't have a suitcase.

"I've got a date tonight," Eleanor said.

"But you'll come back after that," I said, "won't you?"

"I can't," she said. "I have plans all weekend and my own life. And coming back here, even for a few days, would be a step backward. Besides, my bed here's too small for me now."

I didn't really know what she meant by that. Seemed to me, she was still the same exact size she'd been when she moved out.

But I knew my mom had supported Eleanor when Eleanor decided to get her own place. It was what Eleanor wanted, and it was what my mom wanted for her. I supposed I should want it for her, too.

"You'll be fine, squirt," she said, giving me a quick kiss on the forehead. "Bess'll look out for you."

Then she was gone.

I didn't even get a chance to tell her about the Moonwalk Party. Maybe she'd have stayed then. I'd have told her my secret, if I thought it would get her to stay.

And then it was just me and Bess and Campbell, plus Vinny once Bess had gone outside and explained to him that he and Bess needed to stay here with me tonight.

Eleanor had said it would be fine. I wondered if, when she said it, she'd pictured Bess and Vinny smooching on the couch all evening long while I tried to listen to reports of you and Apollo 11 on the TV. So much smooching—I suppose it was fine for Bess and Vinny, but it wasn't so great for me.

Oh, well.

At least I still have Bess.

Sincerely yours,
Mamie

Dear Michael Collins,

When I sealed up yesterday's letter, I thought, *Holy moly!* as Buster would say, because I tell you, it seemed like I might need an even bigger envelope than the large ones I've been using, but somehow I managed.

Today, the newscasters and Buster say that you will reach the moon, or at least enter its orbit, so I know it must be true. You must know it, too.

But here is something you don't know, can't know, because there are no newspapers or newscasters where you are. There is a man named John Fairfax. He just landed his rowboat in Hollywood Beach, which is near Miami, which is in Florida. He left from a place called Gran Canaria, an island off the northwestern coast of Africa, on January 20 of this year. For one hundred and eighty days, he has been at sea on a rowboat named *Britannia* that is only twenty-five feet long. He is the first person ever to row across an ocean solo, which means by himself.

Buster says that when you reach the moon today, that you will be in its orbit and that, eventually, Neil Armstrong and Buzz Aldrin will leave you by yourself when they go down in the *Eagle* to take their walk on the moon, which I hope they get to do. When Buster told me this, I thought that, while they were descending and taking their walk, you would be the loneliest man in the world, all by yourself, orbiting the moon, waiting for them to come back, which I hope they will.

But think about what I just told you, Michael Collins. John Fairfax spent 180 days at sea—*one hundred and eighty days at sea!*—on his lonesome. And yet he survived. It just goes to show that whenever you think you are the loneliest person on the face of the planet—or off it!—there is still yet someone more lonely than you. It is a marvel. It is a marvel and a wonder that anyone survives this world of ours.

But I didn't learn about John Fairfax until later today. Earlier, a bunch of other stuff happened. And once again, much of it was not good.

It started out good, though! When I woke in the morning and remembered again that both my mom and dad are gone and also remembered that, even though she's usually a lot better than Bess, Eleanor hadn't stayed with me either, I told myself I didn't care. I told myself today would be a good day and that I had the excitement ahead of me of planning the Moonwalk Party.

At the thought of that, I raced through my morning routines, not even giving any thought to which cereal I grabbed. Whichever box my hand touched first, that was fine with me.

Okay. It was Froot Loops.

As soon as I was done, I called Buster. It had been over a day since I'd seen him, which is some kind of record for us in the summer unless one of us gets sick or goes on vacation, and I didn't want him to worry that today would be the same as yesterday. But I also wanted him to know that I would be a little later than usual meeting up because I had some things to do first.

"What kind of things?" he asked.

Buster wasn't being nosy. It's just that, with best friends, you can ask each other anything. You can also not answer if you don't want to, no explanation necessary, which is a mighty fine feature. But you can always ask.

Up until then, I'd managed to keep my Moonwalk Party a secret. For an entire day, I'd kept it. But now I found myself wanting to share it with Buster—and anyway, wouldn't he need his mother's permission to come over and watch with me tomorrow night?—so I did.

Buster's excitement at my announcement was satisfying.

"Holy moly! You mean you're going to do the cooking yourself?" he said.

"Uh-huh."

"Holy moly! Will you need me to bring anything?"

I was about to say no, but then I thought of something.

"Do you think you could maybe bring some Tang?" I said.

Yesterday, at the A&P, I'd been so wrapped up in getting food for the party, I hadn't even considered beverages, and there was nothing in the house, not even any Hi-C. Sure, we could drink water, but that would hardly be festive.

"Boy, can I!" Buster said, sounding excited to have something to contribute. "Who's coming to the Moonwalk Party?"

"Well, my mom and dad are still gone." Already this was sounding more like a list of who wasn't coming than who was, but still I felt compelled to add, "And Eleanor just came and went, too—"

"Wait. She's not there anymore? What kind of cavalry is that? Then who's looking out for you?"

I said that Bess was, and for once, someone didn't point out to me how useless that was. Maybe that's because he realized that, right then, she was all I had.

"I'm sure she'll be here," I said, "probably Vinny, too."

"That's okay, then."

"So there's no need to say anything to your mom about my parents being gone," I made sure to add.

"I won't. I still have to ask her if I can come, but I'm sure she'll say yes. So what are you doing now?"

"I just need to make a list, so I've got a schedule of what I need to do and when. After that you can come over."

"You wouldn't rather come here?"

I would. Of course I would. We almost always had a better time at Buster's house than at mine. But somehow, it didn't feel right. I felt like I should stay at home.

"I'm going to have to start some of my preparations today," I said. "If I leave it all for tomorrow, I think it'll be too much to do in one day. Plus, I'm sure we'll want to spend a fair amount of time just staring at the TV, waiting for the astronauts to land."

"True. So what are you going to be preparing today?"

"The cake," I said.

"The *cake*?" Buster said. "You're going to bake a cake in this heat?" Then it was like I could almost see him shrug through the phone. "Okay. What time you want me over?"

"Is a half hour too soon?"

It wasn't, and we hung up.

I had my sheet of notepaper and a pencil out, and was making my timeline on when I'd need to do everything, when I heard a car horn honk outside, honking so many times you'd have thought there was a fire somewhere. I'd gotten out of my chair to go look out the window, but before I could get there, I heard footsteps quickly padding on the floor upstairs, followed by the sounds of more footsteps and something heavier thumping down the stairs. A second later, Bess came into the kitchen, trailing her blue Samsonite luggage behind her.

Never mind that this was the earliest Bess had ever been up on a summer's day unless someone physically dragged her out of bed.

"What's that?" I said, pointing at the Samsonite, hating to ask and scared of the answer.

"My luggage."

"I know that. But where are you going with it?"

Right then, that piece of luggage seemed like everything that's wrong with the world.

"Are we going somewhere?" I asked when she didn't immediately answer, because she'd hauled the luggage up on the kitchen table, opening it and then muttering to herself as she double-checked the contents.

"Me," she said, shutting it, satisfied. "I'm going to Vinny's."

Just like he'd heard his name, the car horn blared again.

"*Vinny's?*"

"Uh-huh," she said. "I'm going over there to watch all the moon stuff with him and his family today and tomorrow . . ." She trailed off, like there might be an endless stream of days ahead after that, before adding, "His parents said it was okay."

"When did you arrange this?" I demanded.

"Last night. After you fell asleep, we talked about it, he called his mom, she said it was okay."

"What about me?"

"You'll be fine here."

"I'm ten!"

Sure, I'd been on my own before. But that was just

the occasional hour or two after school, sometimes longer. It was never like this, though, with everyone going away for who knew how long and no end in sight.

"Call Eleanor, then," she said.

"But she already said she's busy this weekend," I said, but Bess was fiddling with her stuff, so I'm not even sure she heard me. "When will you be back?"

"Who knows?" she said with a shrug, pulling out a pale pink lipstick that was almost white and applying it. "With everyone else gone, there's no sense in my staying around."

No sense?

"What about the party?" I burst out.

That finally stopped her. "What party, runt?" she said, mid-lip-blotting.

"The Moonwalk Party."

"The *what* party?"

So I explained, finishing up with, "And I'm going to bake a cake that's red and white and blue today, and tomorrow I'm going to make the chicken with Campbell's cream of mushroom soup. You've got to stick around for that!"

"Oh, Mamie." When she said those two words, there was so much pity in them that, somehow, it was like the worst thing that had happened to me yet. "You're the only one who thinks that dish is so special. All it really is, though, is plain old chicken and a can of soup."

"What about the cake, then?" I tried, but she was already hefting that Samsonite again and Vinny was already blaring his horn again.

"Will his parents even be there?" I cried desperately. "Will there be *adequate adult supervision*?"

She rolled her eyes at me. "Yes, there will be 'adequate adult supervision.' You're worse than Mom and Dad! I already said we'd be watching all the moon stuff with his family, didn't I? Of *course*, his parents will be there, Mamie. They never go anywhere."

Bess sounded disappointed when she said that last part—so disappointed, I knew it must be true.

"Here." She quickly wrote something at the top of my notepaper. "Vinny's parents' number. Use it if and when our parents come home."

The horn blared again.

"But what about before that?" I yelled after her as she opened the door. "What about me?" I yelled again as she hurried down the path.

"I already told you: call Eleanor," she said over one shoulder. "I'm sure you can talk her into coming home. Once you tell her I've left, she'll have to do it."

"Eleanor said she's too busy this weekend!" I said again, this time at a shout, but it was too late.

Bess was already in the car, and then she was gone.

I thought again, right then and there, of calling my mom at Aunt Jenny's. I would tell her how Eleanor came and went, how Bess just took off to stay at Vinny's parents' house. If I did that, she'd have to come home, wouldn't she? But if I did that, what would it make me? I'll tell you. It would make me a tattletale, that's what.

When you were my age, Michael Collins, was being considered a tattletale just about the worst thing a person could be? Because sometimes it seems like that's the way it is now. Whether it's at home with parents ("Don't tell on your sister—no one likes a tattletale") or at school with teachers (same thing, but replacing "sister" with "classmate"), the message is clear: tattletales are the worst. I'm not sure why that is, why it is worse to tell the truth about the wrong thing someone is doing than the wrong thing is itself, but that is the world I live in. People act like "Don't be a tattletale" is as strict a rule as any of the Ten Commandments—stricter, even! Between you and me, I do not see "Thou shalt not be a tattletale" on any tablets, yet there you have it.

I didn't want to be alone, but I didn't want to be a tattletale either.

One thing I don't think a person can ever truly know, unless of course you carry a mirror around with you at all times, is how we look to other people.

So when Buster came through the door five minutes later, the door that I hadn't even bothered to shut before plopping down at the table after Bess had left, I can't even imagine what I must have looked like to him. Sitting there. My stupid list in front of me now with stupid Vinny's parents' number at the top of it. Tears in my eyes.

No, I don't know what Buster saw when he looked at me right then, but I know what he did. He sat down in the chair closest to mine, and then he did something he'd never done in all our years of best friendship.

He reached out one hand and covered mine with his.

"Mamie," he said softly, "what is it? What's wrong?"

So I told him. I told him about Bess leaving with Vinny. I told him how she was going to miss the Moon-walk Party. I even told him what she'd said about the chicken.

He didn't react as strongly to that last part as you would think. But I suppose we all have our things that rile us up most, and his was this: "How could she leave you here alone?"

"I'm not alone," I said. "Campbell is still here."

"Campbell is a *cat*."

"I know that. But she's still here. Somewhere."

"I don't understand how Bess could leave you alone like this," Buster said. And this was followed by, "You have to let me tell my mom now, Mamie. But it'll be all right. My folks really like you. I'm sure they'll let you come stay with us as long as you need to, until one or both of your parents come back."

If I'd thought I felt panic when Bess first told me she was leaving, that panic getting worse when she left, it was nothing compared to what I felt then.

"*NO!*" I screamed at Buster, something I had never done before, not like that. "You *can't* tell her!"

"How come? It's nothing to be ashamed of. None of this is your fault."

"That's not it."

"Then what, then?"

"If you tell her," I said, "I won't have any choice. I'll *have* to go stay at your house."

I could see Buster struggling not to look offended at this. "I thought you liked it at my house."

"Of course I do," I said. "Most of the time, I like it better than here!"

"Then what, then?" he asked again.

"What if one of them calls?"

Of course, as far as I knew, other than the calls I'd answered from Buster, the phone hadn't rung at all when I was home, unless it was Vinny calling for Bess when she was still here. I supposed it could've rung when I was out in the morning picking up the newspaper from the pavement—I didn't think to take it off the hook when I was doing that. Or even when I was in the bathroom with the door closed and the water running loud because I was brushing my teeth. Maybe not. But maybe.

"What if they call and I'm not here?" I said. "How will any of them be able to find each other again if I'm not here?"

Buster looked at me.

"I don't know." I shrugged. "I don't know why I have to stay here. I just do."

"Okay, then. That's what we'll do." I felt his hand leaving mine. "How can I help?" He didn't wait for an answer. "We were going to make the cake today, right?"

So that's what we did.

I was still a useless puddle, so while I was still being that, Buster rooted around in the cabinets until he found the Betty Crocker white cake mix, which is a great cake to make if you ever have to make one. He studied the instructions on the back of it. Then he set the oven and got out the pans we'd need and the mixer and the other ingredients we'd have to add, like oil and eggs.

By the time he was ready to pour the dry mix into the mixing bowl, I was ready to join him, after setting up the portable fan so we wouldn't get too hot. And then we just worked together side by side. Sometimes I would feel Buster's eyes on me, but he didn't say anything more about the situation with my family, not even when, occasionally, I'd feel a tear tracing its way down my face.

When we were done mixing, and it came time to pour the batter into the pans, we decided to leave more than the usual amount of batter in the bowl for licking later. There was no one to tell us not to, so we enjoyed that as an early lunch during the forty-five minutes it took the cake to bake in the oven. Because of the amount of batter we'd reserved for lunch, the cake came out a little flat and thin, but we didn't mind.

I know I told you how on the Fourth of July, my mom usually sets out red Jell-O next to a white cake with frosting dyed blue. But I figured that since this was my party, I'd improve on that and make the frosting extra special by making it two-toned. Once we'd prepared the icing, added blue food dye to half of it and red food dye to the other half, and then frosted the whole thing, that cake stood up real proud. Or at least, plenty proud enough for us.

Buster asked what else we needed to do to get ready for the party, but I told him nothing. I wanted to do the rest of it myself tomorrow. I wanted for at least some of it to be a surprise to someone.

And then Buster just stayed with me the whole day. We played a rousing game of astronauts, although Campbell was even less a participant than usual.

When it came time for dinner, Buster called his mom for permission to stay and she said yes. I made us each one of the TV dinners Eleanor and I bought yesterday. It turns out Mrs. Whitaker has never bought a TV dinner before either, and Buster agreed with me that with all those compartments, they are just something special.

We watched the news together, which is how I learned about John Fairfax and how we learned for sure that you and the astronauts are at the moon now, orbiting it, so close, having come so far.

Even after it got dark, Buster stayed with me as long as he could. The first time his mom called, he asked if he could stay a little longer and she said yes. But by the third time she called, there was no little longer to be had.

When I asked Buster if he'd come over first thing tomorrow morning, he reminded me about church.

Church? I'd forgotten all about church. But Buster was right. Tomorrow was Sunday.

"You can come with us," Buster offered. "I'm sure my mom will say it's okay, and I won't even tell her about your parents."

So that's the plan we made.

After Buster left, I realized that between church and the party tomorrow, I should take a shower so I could wash my hair and get clean. It seemed like it had been a long time since I'd gotten clean. My mom always says I should be sure someone's nearby when I take a shower, just in case I fall, but I couldn't see any way around it, so off I went, being extra careful not to slip and crack my head, because there would be no one but Campbell to call for an ambulance for me if I did.

Since it was just me, I left the door open a bit, hoping I could hear the sound of the phone over the rushing shower water. After a while, I thought I did hear something, but when I hurriedly turned off the water, I didn't hear a thing. I stood there, shampoo in my hair, hoping so hard that the phone would ring, but it never did.

After I finished my shower, I made sure all the doors were locked and got into bed, but I couldn't really sleep, for thinking about today and tomorrow.

And it was so hot.

That's when I realized something.

No one else was here.

I know, I know, I told you that already. And I certainly know it well enough myself.

But this time when I thought it, it hit me what I could do, and I thought, *To heck with all of them.* I grabbed Campbell up out of my hot bed, went down the hall to my parents' bedroom, turned on the air-conditioning unit in the window, and then lay down on the floor, listening to the hum of it as cool air began to wash over me.

The cat and I just lay side by side, limbs spread out because it was the kind of hot where a person doesn't even want any of her skin to touch any other part of her skin if she can possibly help it. I suppose when you are a cat, the same applies to fur.

I stayed like that all night.

There was no one to say yes. No one to say no.
Who knows, Michael Collins?
Maybe tomorrow, I will have cake for breakfast.

Sincerely yours,
Mamie

Sunday, July 20, 1969

Dear Michael Collins,

I've got to tell you something, and I'm not sure if even you know it yet, but it's this: just when you think the worst thing that could possibly happen happens, something else will happen that's even worse to wipe that right off your radar.

This morning, with no one left here but me and Campbell, I got up, brushed my teeth, and went down for breakfast. Before pouring a hearty bowl of Froot Loops for myself, I opened the back door just to see what the weather was going to be like today.

And that's when it happened.

You may have recalled me telling you about my cat, Campbell, and how she is an indoor cat unless I carry her outside. Well, as soon as I opened the door, she scooted right past me. And even though, as I have perhaps also told you, she has been getting fat and slow, no matter how I chased her, no matter how loud I called for her, after a time I had to admit that I simply could not find her anywhere.

First my mom. Then my dad. Then Eleanor. Then Bess. Now Campbell.

Do you know what happened next, Michael Collins? I will tell you.

I stood in the driveway and screamed.

And what I had to say was:

"What is *wrong* with you people? And cats?"

Followed by:

"DOESN'T ANYBODY STAY WITH THE SHIP ANYMORE???"

That is what I said, Michael Collins, and I am not even ashamed of myself because it is, in the end, simply the truth.

Doesn't anyone stay with the ship anymore?

After my dad left a few days ago, and I shouted in the driveway, I felt so bad afterward that I hurried inside, shutting the door behind me. Now I didn't care who heard me screaming. But I did have to go back inside the house. I needed to get ready so I wouldn't be late for church with Buster's family.

As I neared the door, I could hear the phone ringing. I hurried to pick it up, but of course, of *course*, when I did, only a dial tone was there. I stared at the phone, hoping whoever had tried would call again, but that didn't happen. I was so lonely in that moment, I thought about calling my mom or Eleanor—Bess, even!—but I pushed that idea away. They left *me*. If they cared, they could call *me*. Still, I stared at the phone a moment longer, hoping. Eventually I had to just give up and go get dressed.

I was so worried for Campbell, I had to keep brushing tears away as I looked for something appropriate to wear. But then I decided to push the worry somewhere deep inside myself where no one could see it. If Buster's mom saw me with tears all over my face, she'd be bound to start asking questions. And if I started talking, who knew what might come out of my mouth?

So I went on autopilot again. You know what I'm talking about.

As I went through the items in my closet and drawers, nothing looked right to me. Everything looked so babyish: the dresses with lace collars and other stupid stuff. I wanted something better than that, more grown-up. I wanted something in red and white and blue to honor what was going to happen later. That's when I got the idea of raiding my mom's closet.

Normally, Michael Collins, I would not go in there, and I certainly would never take her things, not without permission. But there was no one here for me to ask, and

I'm sure you will agree and forgive me when I say: I am no longer living in normal times.

As soon as I pulled the metal cord on the overhead lightbulb, I knew I'd made the right decision. For there, hanging right in front of me, was a pencil skirt in the reddest of reds. When I put it on, of course it was too big for me, too long and so loose in the waist that it fell right down off my hips. And because it was getting so close to leaving time, I couldn't hem it or take it in at the waist—not that I'm much good with a needle and thread; whenever I've tried to make an outfit for one of my dolls from discarded fabric, it has never come out quite as planned.

But that was okay! I just folded that skirt a couple of times at the waistband, and that raised it right up—plus all the folding made it tighter at the waist. When I found a belt to hold the folds in place and cinched it together, you could barely see any lumpy bunching. For a shirt, I found the perfect thing: one of my mom's sleeveless, button-down linen shirts she wears in the summer with Bermuda shorts. This one was in the purest white. And if it was a little big, too, again, so what? At least it would cover any bunches still at my waist from the skirt. And then, for navy blue, I grabbed one of my headbands, and I even took the time to position it right so that there were no stray clumps of hair in odd places.

Finally, I briefly considered taking a pair of my mom's high heels. They'd never fit, but I could always put some tissue paper in the toes like I used to do when I was younger and liked to play wedding. But I immediately rejected that idea. I didn't want to look like I was trying too hard. Besides, Keds really do go with everything. They are just fantastic like that.

Then, I went and stared at the phone again, willing it to ring, right up until Buster knocked for me, wearing his navy-blue church suit and telling me that it was time. I told him about Campbell taking off on me, too, and I could see the immediate concern on his face, but we didn't even have time to discuss it because his parents were waiting in the car. A part of me wanted to tell him to go on without me—I was sure that whoever had called would try again—but I couldn't do that. Some things you have to leave home for. And I just couldn't miss church. Not today. I had to go and pray for you.

So I took the phone off the hook and went outside with Buster.

"That's an, um, *interesting* outfit you have on," Mrs. Whitaker said when I climbed in the car with Buster.

"Thank you, ma'am," I said.

"How come you're not going to church with your own family today?"

"Because they're, um"—I figured if "um" could work for her, it could work for me too—"getting ready."

This was not, strictly speaking, a lie. Wherever they were, they had to be getting ready for something. Aren't people always?

"Oh?" she said, a question.

"We're having a Moonwalk Party tonight," I said.

So what if this was in no way connected to whatever my parents might be getting ready for. This was also still a true statement. Our house *was* having a Moonwalk Party tonight!

"It was nice of you to invite Buster to that," she said. "We're having one, too. Isn't it exciting?"

I agreed that it was.

"At least since we're both having parties," she said gaily, "neither house will get upset at the noise the other house is making."

I agreed that this was true, too, although somehow I doubted our house would be as noisy as theirs.

I have to tell you, going to a church you are not accustomed to is a strange thing. Sure, I recognized some kids from school at Buster's family's church. Some kids from school go to my family's church, too, although, obviously, not the same kids who go to Buster's. But the way the church was decorated was different, and the tunes to the hymns were different. Even what people stood up for and sat down for were different, so much so that I found myself constantly struggling not to fall too far off the tempo. And, of course, the preacher was different.

"Let us bow our heads and pray," the preacher said. "Our Heavenly Father, we ask that you protect those three brave men, that you guide Neil Armstrong and Edwin Aldrin down to the moon and back again, and that you return all three astronauts safely back to Earth. We ask this in your name. Amen."

I tried not to hold it against the preacher that he didn't mention you specifically by name. To him, you were just one of "all three astronauts." Well, you and I both know you're better than that.

As I looked around the church at the people there, praying for you, it occurred to me that across the country, maybe even the whole planet, just about everyone alive, no matter what their religion, must be praying for your safety today. I wondered if my dad was one of those people. When you lifted off a few days ago, that look

I saw on his face—I think he saw something in that moment that he had never seen before. So I think he, too, must be praying for you now, Michael Collins. I'm almost sure of it.

After praying with everyone else for the astronauts, I said a silent prayer to myself for Campbell. I hope you don't think that's wrong—putting a cat so high up there with people—but she is just a little girl cat and now she is alone out there in the world. Plus, she was the only family member I had left when I got up this morning.

When the car pulled into Buster's driveway a short time after leaving church, Mrs. Whitaker leaned over the seat to look back at me.

"Would you like to stay for Sunday dinner, Mamie?" she asked.

Oh, how I would have liked to say yes! Just thinking about all that Sunday dinner could entail—probably some kind of roast, definitely mashed potatoes, a green vegetable that hopefully wasn't too horrible and wouldn't be if it was swimming in butter, and maybe pie or ice cream for dessert; maybe even both pie *and* ice cream. Thinking about it made my mouth water. Plus, thinking about it made me realize how long it had been since an adult had made a proper meal for me. Well, Eleanor made me that cold chicken salad, but that hardly felt like the same thing now. Still, tempting as it was, I couldn't accept.

"Thank you, ma'am," I said, "but no thank you." I opened the car door and stepped out. "I need to go get ready for the party tonight. Thank you for taking me to church."

"You're welcome, Mamie. What time would you like Buster over?"

"Seven o'clock would be good!" I said, and turning to my best friend, added, "See you then, Buster!"

And then I was slamming the door shut and running through the stand of trees separating our properties.

Before going inside, I searched all over for Campbell again, but to no avail.

Once inside, I went and put the phone in the kitchen back on the hook. Right then and there, I decided that whatever was going to happen with the phone was going to happen, and there wasn't a single thing I could do about that.

I turned on the portable fan and started looking for the fancy toothpicks, the ones with colorful frilly cellophane on the edges, to use later on with the cocktail franks. The phone rang, but it was Buster, telling me all about the *Eagle* undocking from the *Columbia*.

Remember when I started keeping track of the days and I told you that I might even start keeping track of the minutes, too? Well, here it is, Michael Collins. Every minute is important now.

Today, at 1:47 p.m., the *Eagle*, carrying Neil Armstrong and Buzz Aldrin in it, began the journey to the surface of the moon, leaving you by yourself in the *Columbia*.

"They said so on TV," Buster said.

I told him to hang on for a minute. Then I dropped the phone so it clattered and ran to turn on the TV. But there was nothing to see, just men talking over a simulation.

I ran back to the phone, snatched it up.

"I wish we could see it," I said, sighing.

"I know," Buster said. "But they say Neil Armstrong has some kind of camera he'll attach to the outside of the *Eagle* and then we'll be able to see everything, once they get to the moon."

"Which they hopefully will," I said.

"Hopefully," he agreed.

I wondered what you were thinking then, Michael Collins. Were you wishing you could go with them, or had you somehow found a way to be happy right where you were?

"How is it even possible," I said, my mind moving on to something else, "for a little spacecraft to land on something like the moon when the moon's always moving, too?"

"You need to aim ahead of it," Buster said, "so the moon's own speed can catch you at the right moment. That's how you intercept it."

"How long do you think it'll take," I asked, "them getting there?"

"A few hours still," he said. "That's what they said on TV."

"Okay," I said, "then I'd better get on with my cleaning."

"Okay."

It's amazing how long it takes to clean a house all by yourself. But you can't have a party in a dirty house. So I just got to it. I put on an apron so I wouldn't get my pretty outfit dirty, and then I dusted and vacuumed and polished and straightened. I even did something about the bathrooms, although, I must confess, not much.

Then I started decorating. There wasn't a lot, just some red and white and blue streamers left over from the Fourth of July. I used those in the dining room and living room. I also found a couple of red-white-and-blue cocktail napkins in a pack and put those out, too. If we were careful with them, maybe we could make them last the night.

A few hours later, the phone rang again.

Each time the phone rang, I was disappointed that it wasn't anyone in my family calling, but also glad that at least I still had Buster.

"They did it!" Buster cried, excited. "They're on the moon!"

"Oh, no!" I cried back, disappointed. "You mean they walked on the moon already and I missed it?"

"No, that won't come until later. But at four-eighteen p.m., the *Eagle* landed in the Sea of Tranquility."

"They landed in a sea?" What was Buster talking about? "Is that even safe?"

"No. I mean, yes, it's safe. But no, it's not really a sea. There's no water on the moon, Mamie. Just a flat plain where they are now. They just name all the places on the moon different things. It doesn't have to make linguistic sense."

"Oh. Well. How soon will they be walking?"

"No one knows." He paused, then: "Do you want me to come over sooner than seven? Just in case?"

I felt a *Phew!* run through me over things I hadn't even known I'd been feeling.

"Could you?" I asked.

"Sure," he said. "When do you want me?"

I thought about this.

"Now?" I said.

Buster arrived so quickly, it practically qualified as magic.

He stood there on the other side of the door, holding his pitcher of Tang. Buster had on his navy-blue suit and tie and a stiff white shirt, just like he'd had on when we went to church that morning, only now there was something in his hair, slicking it down.

"You still have your suit on?" I said.

"Not still," he said. "I took it off when I got home, but then I put it back on again." He shrugged. "Well, it is a party."

"What's that in your hair?" I asked.

"Vitalis. Do you like it?"

I wasn't sure how I felt about it.

"It's different," I finally said. Then I remembered my manners and invited him in.

"The place looks great," he said as I took the pitcher of Tang from him and set it down. Then he walked around some, like he'd never been here before. "I really like what you did with these decorations," he said when he got to the dining room.

"Would you like some hors d'oeuvres?" I asked. "I can get those started."

"That'd be great."

So I boiled the cocktail franks in water, remembering to turn off the burner when they were cooked, put them on a plate, stuck party toothpicks in them. Then I poured chips into a bowl and stirred together sour cream and French onion soup mix to make the dip in another bowl, because, as I believe I may have mentioned in a previous letter, you can't have a party without chips and dip.

Then I brought it all out into the living room and set it up on the coffee table so we could keep an eye on the TV, although there wasn't much to see yet: just a lot of people talking and a bunch of maps and charts and more simulations.

That was okay, though, because Buster had ideas about everything.

"Today when Armstrong and Aldrin exited the *Columbia* into the *Eagle*, Michael Collins pressed a button causing the two crafts to separate. Then Aldrin fired the rockets on the *Eagle*, and off they went."

"How do they even guide the *Eagle* to get it precisely on the moon?" I asked.

"Rockets." Buster shrugged. "Radar. The *Eagle* has

sixteen small rockets around it to help position it: up, down, left, right. Hey, these franks are good!"

"Thanks. Just be careful with that cocktail napkin. It's got to last you through all of the courses."

Buster's eyes widened. "You mean we're having even more than this?"

"Uh-huh. Which reminds me. I better go start my chicken."

"Do you need any help?"

"Nah, you'd better stay here so you can call me if anything happens."

There's not much that my sister Bess is ever right about, but I'll tell you, it turned out she was right about that chicken. In order to make it with the Campbell's cream of mushroom soup, all you do is set the oven, place pieces of chicken in a pan, open up the can of soup, pour it over the chicken, and then put the whole thing in the oven to bake. So nothing hard. I suppose for something to be considered special, it has to be hard or at least rare. But you know what? I don't care. Even though I know the trick of it now, somehow that chicken is still special to me.

While it baked in the oven, the house getting hotter and hotter as a result, and me not sure what to do with the portable fan—leave it in the kitchen where the hot oven was or put it in the living room where the hot "we" were—I asked Buster, "Don't you want to take your jacket off?"

"Can I?" he said, clearly relieved. "Tie, too?" He was already tugging at the knot.

"Knock yourself out."

Honestly, he looked good in his suit, but I didn't want him to suffer for the sake of beauty.

When the chicken was ready and still nothing new was happening on TV, I decided to serve us in the dining room, on the good dishes and things like I had with my sisters two days ago. Just to be on the safe side, I turned the volume on the TV in the living room up as high as it would go so we wouldn't miss anything.

As soon as we started eating, Buster got awful quiet.

"Is the chicken okay?" I asked.

"It's great." He took another bite. "My mom never makes anything like this. How do you make it? Maybe you could give her the recipe."

"Oh, it's real easy," I said, and told him how I did it.

"Huh," he said. "I don't think my mom's ever made anything with a can of soup before. Well, except soup."

Then he fell quiet again.

All that could be heard was the sound of the TV blaring and, over that, noises coming through the windows from the party at his house.

"Do you wish you were there?" I said. "At your parents' party?"

I thought for sure that must be it. It sounded so big and like everyone was having a good time.

"Oh, no," he said. "I'm fine where I am. It's just . . ."

"Just what?"

"It's like this. You look forward to something happening, you even dream about it. But dreaming and doing are two different things. When you're actually doing, there's still so much that could go wrong."

He may be my closest friend, the person I know best in this world, but sometimes the things that come out of Buster's mouth, they are a puzzle.

"What are you talking about, Buster?"

"The astronauts, of course."

That's when it hit me. For the first time, Buster was worried. And if he was worried, what hope did I have?

Still, I had to ask him. "They made it, Buster. They're on the moon. What could go wrong now?"

"What couldn't? Take those spacesuits of theirs. Each spacesuit is like a mini pressurized spacecraft. It's got a radio and its own oxygen supply. There are lunar gloves, lunar overshoes—you name it. Helmets with visors because of the sun's light. A backpack with more oxygen in it—and there's no gravity, so it's actually easy to carry it all."

"Then what's the problem?"

"No one really knows what will happen when they step out onto the moon. No one's ever done this before! There could be dangers."

"Like?"

"Like if they get a hole in one of those suits while outside of the ship? Blood and body fluids would come to a boil. You'd blow up like a balloon and suffocate."

I could feel my mouth falling open as I thought about this. Then: "Aw, that won't happen. I'll bet they tested those things a million times." All the while I was thinking: *Well, at least you, Michael Collins, don't have to worry about that happening to you.*

"Still."

"What do you think they're doing right now?" I asked, to change the subject, to get Buster's mind off things—mine, too. "What do you think is taking so long?"

"They have to make sure the *Eagle* will be ready for takeoff again. Before they can even leave it at all, they have to make sure the *Eagle* is ready, in case they have to depart suddenly."

"What about Michael Collins?" I said. "What do you think he's doing right now?"

"Spinning. Waiting. The *Columbia* has to keep spinning. Otherwise, it would get too hot from the sun striking the same side all the time, and then it would burn up. He's spinning and orbiting the moon while he waits for them to come back. It takes him two hours to orbit. And for half of each orbit, when he's on the far side of the moon and therefore turned away from Earth, there's no radio contact at all."

Somehow, that idea felt too big for my brain. So I didn't think about it, not just then.

Instead, I got up to clear the dishes.

Buster stopped me. "I'll get those," he said. "You cooked. It's only fair."

So that's what happened. Buster cleared and washed all the dishes, while I went into the living room, sat down on the couch, and put my feet up like a lady of leisure. It did occur to me that if my dad always did the dishes after my mom cooked, like Buster was doing right now, my mom might appreciate that fact. And now that I'd taught my dad how to wash dishes, maybe he might do that someday. If they ever came back.

Not long after the sound of running water stopped, Buster came in with forks and big slices of the cake we made together yesterday, all set out on plates. We ate those and had seconds. I'd forgotten to make the Jell-O, but a person can't always remember everything.

And then you know what we did, Michael Collins? We just watched and waited. Picture a big clock on the wall, the minute hand sweeping round and round while the hour hand goes more slowly.

It's a funny thing about waiting for something for a real long time. No matter how worried or scared or even flat-out excited you are because of all the things that still might happen, tiredness gets you. In the end, it was all I could do to keep awake and it felt like, if it wouldn't be so painful, I could have sure used some of those fancy toothpicks to prop my eyelids open. And Buster looked the same.

But then, just as I was about to drift off, it happened.

"Holy moly!" Buster cried.

And just for once, I said "Holy moly!" right along with him, because there, running as a caption along the bottom of the Magnavox color TV screen, it now read, in words that it would have been impossible to imagine before: *LIVE VOICE OF ASTRONAUT ARMSTRONG FROM SURFACE OF MOON*. I'd seen *Live from Ohio* and *Live from Paris* and even *Live from Vietnam* and *Live from* almost any other place you can imagine, but no one had ever seen this before, what people were seeing on television screens across the country, the world even:

LIVE . . . FROM SURFACE OF MOON

There was Neil Armstrong—shadowy, but still, there he was—backing down the steps of the *Eagle*. The legs of the *Eagle* looked like they were covered in tinfoil as he backed down the steps still separating him from the moon. Nine steps, to be exact. I know because I counted them. And when he got to the bottom, he placed a foot on the moon.

At 10:56 p.m. today, on July 20, 1969, for the first time ever, a man put a foot on the moon.

I tell you, Michael Collins, Buster and I were wide-awake now.

We were awake to hear Neil Armstrong say, as he set that first foot down, "That's one small step for man, one giant leap for mankind."

I tell you something else, Michael Collins. Buster always says that you can learn anything in the world from books, and I know he's right. You can. Certainly, there are a lot of words in books. But there aren't words, not really, to describe what it is like to witness a miracle firsthand.

A man, Michael Collins. On the moon.

There are facts, and facts don't begin to cover it, but I will try to tell you what some of them were, since you are one of the few people who was not able to see this on the TV tonight. I may get the order of some of the facts wrong, but that is because there was so much excitement and so much happened and I am finishing this letter so late.

Walter Cronkite said, "Armstrong is on the moon. Neil Armstrong—thirty-eight-year-old American—standing on the surface of the moon!"

I felt Buster's hand close over mine.

We watched as Neil Armstrong took pictures with a camera, collected rocks and samples to bring back, and set up experiments for scientists at home. For about twenty minutes, Neil Armstrong was the only man walking on the moon, the only man who had ever walked there. Then finally, at 11:15 p.m., Buzz Aldrin joined him.

Once they were together, they put up an American flag and Buzz Aldrin saluted it. It looked like it was quite a struggle to get it right, and Walter Cronkite said it had wire sewn into it to keep it stiff, because otherwise it would just hang straight down, limp, with no wind to buoy it.

Buzz Aldrin tried to run but wound up just bouncing all over the place like a kangaroo. They both did.

"You see those footprints they're leaving?" Buster said. "There's no rain or wind on the moon. Their footprints will be there forever."

But not yours, Michael Collins.

Then President Nixon called—in a telephone-radio transmission from the Oval Office of the White House to the surface of the moon—to congratulate the astronauts and to say, "For one priceless moment in the whole history of man, all the people on this Earth are truly one. One in their pride in what you have done. And one in our prayers that you will return safely to Earth."

I suppose I should have paid more attention to that last part of what President Nixon said, but I didn't. Things were happening too quickly now. There was too much to see.

Neil Armstrong and Buzz Aldrin put up a plaque. It said:

HERE MEN FROM THE PLANET EARTH
FIRST SET FOOT UPON THE MOON

JULY 1969, A. D.

WE CAME IN PEACE FOR ALL MANKIND

I have to tell you, I liked that it said "men from the planet Earth" instead of "American men from the planet Earth." I liked that it just says "men," no country specified, even if sometimes it feels like we've been competing in the space race with the Russians forever. It did have President Nixon's signature at the bottom, with "President, United States of America" under that, but it didn't seem to me like that part mattered as much as the rest.

For two and a half hours, Buster and I watched this miracle together. At moments, I wondered if my various family members, wherever they each were now, were watching, too. Were they seeing exactly what I saw? And if so, what did they think of it all?

And then Armstrong and Aldrin climbed back into their four-legged spider, the lunar module, the *Eagle*. Right before getting back inside, they jettisoned their backpacks from the top of the nine-step staircase.

"What are they doing that for?" I said.

"They don't need them anymore," Buster said. "They'll spend the night on the moon, sleeping in the *Eagle*, before trying to meet up with Michael Collins tomorrow."

I should have thought more about that "trying," just like I should have thought more about President Nixon's "return safely," but somehow I didn't. Instead, I was thinking about Armstrong and Aldrin leaving their backpacks on the moon, about how right since liftoff you'd been getting rid of parts and things once they were no longer needed. It made me think again about what my dad had said about Apollo 11 not even being reusable, and how he'd made that sound bad. But so what if it wasn't? So what if they kept casting parts aside once those items were no longer required? They'd needed it all, every last piece of it, to work properly together in order to get to where they wanted to be.

With the best part over, I turned off the TV. And then, without even discussing it with each other first, Buster and I went outside. We hadn't noticed, but while we were watching, it had rained and the ground was all wet. It was also cooler.

Immediately, I began calling for Campbell, thinking if she'd been caught in the rain, for sure she'd want to come inside to get her feet dry even though the rain had stopped. Buster yelled for her, too, but nothing.

"I'm sure she's fine," he said, sounding confident.

"I'm sure, too," I said, even though I wasn't.

"Just a second," Buster said, racing over to his house, from where I could still hear the sound of the party.

When he came back, he had a beach blanket and he laid it on the ground.

"Here," he said. "You don't want to get your outfit all wet and dirty."

I actually didn't care about my outfit at that point, yet it made me feel good that he cared about it, for my sake.

Sometimes, I feel like I should tell you more about Buster than I do. But the fact of the matter is, Michael Collins, that Buster is just *good*, like you, and that's all there is.

You know how good he is? I think that, all night, even though he knew how happy I was to have him there, he also knew how much I missed my family. So right then, he gave me a gift out of the blue. Buster told me his real name, Michael Collins! I would love to tell you what it is. It is just as purely awful as promised. But I gave my word, and I have to keep my friend's confidence. Some things I can't tell even you, Michael Collins.

After that, we just lay there, side by side, thinking our own thoughts as we stared up at the moon, now that the rain was over and the clouds were gone. The moon was so much different to us now than it had been even the day before, so much different than it would ever be again. We lay like that until Buster's mom started calling for him, later than she'd ever had to.

Then Buster was gone.

And I just stayed out in the backyard for a bit, me, alone, looking up at the moon, thinking about you spinning around it, alone. I hope the *Columbia* is spinning like it's supposed to, so that it doesn't get too hot from the sun, because then you would burn up and die. I hope that for the half of each orbit during which you are on the far side of the moon and therefore turned away from the Earth—and so are unable even to have any radio contact—you do not feel too alone. Has any man ever been more alone in the history of the world? Maybe John Fairfax in his rowboat. But other than him? Really, I hope you do not feel too alone.

Because you know what?

You give us hope.

After tonight, there will still be bad things going on all over the world. There will still be Vietnam. There will still be the race riots. There will still be all kinds of bad things. Even in my own house. But you and the other astronauts, tonight you give us hope that miracles can happen and things can get better and we can all come together to want the same good thing.

You give us hope.
Sleep tight, Michael Collins. Sleep tight.

Sincerely yours,
Mamie

Monday, July 21, 1969

Dear Michael Collins,

There's something about a house without other people in it, not even a cat. When other people are there, even if those people are sleeping, it just feels different somehow, fuller. But when it's only you, everything is just so quiet.

When I went downstairs for breakfast and opened the cabinet for the cereal, I was about to reach for the Froot Loops when something changed my mind. For some reason I felt that, even with no one else there looking, no one else to see, I should just eat the Cap'n Crunch instead, like my mom would want me to do.

So that's what I did.

And I'll tell you something, Michael Collins. For the first time it occurred to me that Cap'n Crunch has sugar in it, too. So I don't really know anymore what my mom has against Froot Loops.

But you know what? This is no day for sadness. Yesterday, man walked on the moon for the first time. And today? Here are the headlines from the *New York Times*:

MEN WALK ON MOON

ASTRONAUTS LAND ON PLAIN;
COLLECT ROCKS, PLANT FLAG

The way they put it, it hardly sounds very impressive. But believe me, I watched it all, and it was.

I had no time to worry about the *Times*, though, because, not even bothering to call first, Buster was right there, knocking on my door.

"What's wrong?" I said, thinking that for him to be coming so early without calling first, something new had to be wrong.

Only it wasn't.

"Come on!" Buster said, taking my hand, pulling me outside and dragging me toward the stand of trees so abruptly, I didn't get a chance to put any shoes on or even take the phone off the hook.

"What is it?" I asked, running to keep up with him and to keep from falling as he pulled me.

But all Buster would say was "Holy moly! You've got to see this!"

And then we were in Buster's backyard, standing at the edge of the hole the men had dug for the swimming pool, and there, down in the shallow end, was a cat, with furry little kittens all around her.

"It's Campbell!" Buster cried.

It most surely was.

I don't know that I've ever felt more relieved in my life. Campbell was okay! And those tiny kittens! I suppose you could say that calling kittens cute is a cliché, but what else are you going to call them?

"How did you find her?" I asked.

"When I came out a little while ago, I thought to look for her for you. It's early, so the neighborhood's still quiet, and I guess some people are sleeping in after the excitement last night, so it was easy to notice any little sound. That's when I heard the mewing. I followed the mewing, and there she was!"

Wow.

"We can't leave her there," Buster said. "It's not safe. It's amazing predators haven't gotten to them already."

You know, sometimes when Buster shares his extensive knowledge of things like science with me, like when he tells me all the ways you and the others might die, it does occur to me that he has too much knowledge. But then, when it comes to knowing about things like dangers to Campbell and her kittens posed by predators, that knowledge does come in handy.

I looked all around, ready to fight off a wolf or whatever might try to come their way.

"What do we do?" I asked. I'd never had a cat have kittens before, and I didn't think I was supposed to just lift up the little tiny newborns and carry them away like that.

"I don't know," Buster said. "I'll go wake up my mom." He was off before I could think to stop him.

A few minutes later, he was back with Mrs. Whitaker, who was wearing her summer bathrobe tight around herself, looking even more tired after her party than I felt after mine, her black hair for once out of shape and only the remnants of her Cleopatra eyes still there.

"Now, why would Campbell have gone there to have her babies?" Mrs. Whitaker said, looking at them down there in the shallow end of the hole. "That's not what a cat would normally do."

"I don't know, ma'am," I said, not thinking to choose my words carefully. "Maybe home just didn't feel like home to her anymore."

Mrs. Whitaker just stared at me. Well, of course she did. But all she said was "Wait here."

She hurried to the house, coming back a minute later with a big soft blanket. Then, not even worrying about getting dirty, she climbed into that hole, laid down the blanket, and slid Campbell and her kittens onto it, moving them like they were just one piece. Then we got in there with her and, each taking a part of the blanket so we formed a triangular sling, we carefully lifted them out and carried them back to my house.

When we were there and had set them up in something more comfortable than a dirty hole, Mrs. Whitaker gazed down at them. The "something more comfortable" was a large drawer I'd pulled out of my dresser, dumping all the clothes out on the floor and then placing another soft blanket inside.

"They sure are cute," she said.

"That they are," I said.

She opened her mouth to say something more, but she just stopped. Then she put her head to one side, listening. And I knew what she was hearing: the sound of a house that's empty of everyone but you.

It really is an unmistakable sound.

I thought she must know then, that there wasn't anyone living here anymore other than me. Well, and now Campbell again and her kittens. I thought for sure she'd say something about it. And what would I do then? How would I argue with her if she said I couldn't stay here anymore, not without adult supervision? Already, I was coming up with arguments in my head, or trying to.

But all she said, as she looked me in the eye, was "Are you okay here, Mamie?"

"I'm fine," I said. I raised my chin. "I'm just fine."

"Okay, then," she said after a long minute. "But you be sure to call me if you need anything."

"I'll do that. Thank you, ma'am."

After giving Campbell a pat on the head and telling her, "You've done a good job," Mrs. Whitaker left, and it was just me and Buster and the kittens.

We lay on the floor, across from each other, watching Campbell and the kittens between us.

"Last night sure was something," Buster said.

"And how," I agreed. "Thank goodness that's all over with and I don't have to worry anymore."

"What do you mean?"

Wasn't it obvious?

"Well," I said, "when the astronauts lifted off the other day, there was always the worry that they could die right there on the launchpad. Then the worry about them flying to the moon and the million other things that could still go wrong. Then all the things you told me last night about the spacesuits. But they made it. No more worrying."

"Of course there's still stuff to worry about, Mamie."

I looked at him real sharp then. "What are you talking about, Buster?"

That's when Buster told me that in addition to takeoffs being one of the most dangerous parts of flight, landings are equally to be feared, not to mention everything that could go wrong in between. I don't know how that had never occurred to me before, particularly after President Nixon said that part to the astronauts about praying they returned safely. I'd just been so focused on you all simply getting there, to the moon.

I think now maybe it's because the human brain can only keep so many bad possibilities in it at one time. It's like with my family being gone. Am I worried and upset? Sure. But I can't think about it every second of the day. I have to take care of things, and I have to live—laugh even.

But now here was Buster, telling me about everything that could still go wrong today. Of course, he'd only hinted at the dangers before. But now? He got more specific.

"What if the rockets fail to ignite and the *Eagle* fails to lift off again?" he said. "They die. Because if they don't lift off, they only have enough oxygen left for one more day. And if they lift off, but they make a mistake and miss docking with the command module? They could just drift away, and no one would ever see them again. Well, except for each other. And only that until they die. Even if they do successfully dock again with the *Columbia*? They'll have moon dust all over them. No one knows what that'll do when mixed with oxygen. Will it catch fire? But the astronauts need oxygen, so—"

"So you're telling me they could still die at any time until they re-dock."

"Uh-huh."

"And Michael Collins could still have to come back alone?"

"Uh-huh."

"Is there any more I need to know?"

"Yes. But I have a feeling you don't want to know it just yet."

"You're right. I don't."

Do you see what I mean about Buster?

Honestly, Michael Collins. I thought it was just going to be smooth sailing from here on in until you get back to Earth.

And you know what, it was. Or at least this stage was. Because later on today we got word that the *Eagle* ascended just fine and re-docked with you just fine and you're all heading on home, scheduled to land back here in just two and a half days.

"Now do you want to know the rest of it?" Buster asked, once we'd learned about the re-docking going smoothly.

I put my hands over my eyes as if shutting off my own sight would somehow make it so I didn't have to hear.

"Fine," I said, though with a groan. "Tell me."

"When they reach Earth again and reenter Earth's atmosphere, the outside of the craft will heat up to twenty-five times hotter than a kitchen oven. The craft is protected by a special heat shield that's coated with resin that burns away while keeping it cool. They'll be traveling at nearly twenty-five thousand miles per hour. But they'll need to slow down drastically, because other-wise?"

"They'll die."

"Too steep a reentry? They burn up and—"

"Die."

"Too shallow? Never get a second chance and they—"

"Die."

"Have to get it just right while going nearly twenty-five thousand miles per hour so that, oh, even in perfect conditions, they'll become a fireball."

"Oh, is that all?"

"There are parachutes that'll come out to slow their descent. But if those parachutes don't deploy at exactly the right time and in exactly the right way?"

"They die."

"That's right. The *Columbia* would hit the water with such velocity, the astronauts would be killed on impact."

"So, basically, they could still die at any moment."

"Pretty much."

Oh, why did I let Buster tell me all about that? And why did you let yourself get into this mess, Michael Collins? Did you know all this when you started?

I tell you, I sure didn't. I thought getting to the moon was the whole deal. I sure should have been paying more attention to the "return safely" part. My dad always says President Nixon isn't worth listening to. This time, at least, it would appear my dad is wrong.

But you know what? And this may sound crazy to you, but I *can't* worry about all that right now. I just can't worry about anything, period.

I've got Campbell back, and her and her kittens to think about.

I haven't named them all yet, since I don't know, if or when anyone else comes home, whether I'll be allowed to keep them all. But I did name one. I named him Michael

Collins. I hope you don't mind. I hope you don't feel insulted, having a cat named after you.

If it helps any, let me just tell you this about Michael Collins the cat:

He is the best one.

Sincerely yours,
Mamie

Dear Michael Collins,

Yesterday, two great things happened: (1) I found Campbell and her kittens and brought them back home; and (2) the *Eagle* successfully re-docked with the *Columbia*, and now all three of you astronauts are heading back to Earth.

Well, today a third great thing happened. I have to say, I am surprising even myself by putting it like that, and you will know what I'm talking about when I tell you what it is: Bess came home today.

I never would have guessed before that seeing Bess would make me feel so happy, but such is this endlessly surprising world of ours in which wonders never cease.

"Did you break up with Vinny?" I said.

"No," she said.

"Did Vinny break up with you?" I said.

"No," she said.

"Well, then, did the two of you get in a fight?"

"No," she said.

"Then what, then? Why'd you come back?"

"I just missed you, I guess." She looked around. "Also, Mrs. Whitaker called and told me I better come home or else."

"Mrs. Whitaker?"

I tried to figure out what must have happened. Maybe when Buster got home last night, she grilled him and he finally caved to the pressure?

A part of me wanted to be mad at him, but really, how could I? Buster had kept my secret for as long as he could, and when he simply couldn't keep it any longer, he'd chosen the path of least resistance: Bess. How he got Vinny's number, I don't know, but Buster is nothing if not resourceful.

As for Mrs. Whitaker, it was actually kind of nice to think that at least one of the adults in my acquaintance could still act like a grown-up.

"You never called Eleanor?" Bess said now.

"Campbell had kittens," I said, by way of an answer.

"That's nice," she said. And then she yawned. "I think I'll take a nap."

Well, it was only ten in the morning. She must have felt cheated out of half a night's sleep.

"Okay, then," I said.

And it was. It was most definitely okay to have her back.

After she went upstairs, I called Buster and he came right over.

"How'd your mom get Vinny's parents' phone number?" I asked once he was inside.

"It was right at the top of your notepad," he said, "the one with the list for the party. I saw it and memorized it, and then I gave it to her when she asked what was going on. I figured she'd know what to do."

Just as I'd suspected.

"And you just told her? You told your mom what's been going on?"

"I had to, Mamie," he said. "She'd been asking all kinds of questions. She knew something here wasn't right."

"How'd she know that?"

"Gosh, Mamie, my mom's not an idiot! I know a lot of folks in the neighborhood think she is, but she's just not. You coming to church with us, there being no cars in your driveway two nights ago even though you were supposed to be throwing this big party, all kinds of little things."

"So you told."

"I couldn't lie to her. And anyway, I was worried about you, Mamie. I still am."

I thought then, when he said that, that what he'd done wasn't at all like tattling, not even a little bit. Also, who knew Mrs. Whitaker's "or else" could be so powerful?

And you know what, Michael Collins? I'm still not thinking about all those things Buster said could go wrong on reentry.

No, I'm not thinking about any of that.

At all.

Sincerely yours,

Mamie

Dear Michael Collins,

You know how when you think something can't get worse, that there can't be anything new to worry about, and then there is? Well, sometimes, when things start getting better and you think that's going to be all there is and that's okay—like Campbell getting found with her kittens and Bess coming home, too—things can still get better.

When I heard a car door slam in the driveway, I thought it must be Vinny coming for Bess as usual. It was so nice having even her back, I was ready to beg her not to leave me alone again.

But when I looked at her, she said, "Don't look at me."

So then, hope against hope, I thought maybe it might be my mom or my dad. I ran to the door and outside.

Well, it wasn't.

But it was something almost as good as that.

This is by way of saying that when the day was almost over, a little after five in the afternoon, Eleanor came home.

"What are you doing here?" I cried.

"Folks home yet?" she asked, by way of not answering.

"Not yet," I said.

"Well, then." She went around to the back of her car, popped the trunk, and pulled out a suitcase. "I've come to stay for a bit. I tried to call last night to tell you I'd be here today, but all I got was a busy signal."

Bess.

"But what about your work?" I said, remembering what she'd said. "What about your life? You said that's why you couldn't stay before."

"I'll still have those. I can drive to work from here as easily as I can from my apartment."

"But what about you saying that coming back home was like taking a step backward? What about your bed here not being big enough for you?" I asked, remembering the other things she'd said.

"It'll be okay for a little while," she said. "Maybe I can get some thinking done while I'm here. And it's not like it's going to be forever."

No. I guess I'd known that. Although who knows? Maybe if our parents never come back, it will have to be.

"Can I help you with that?" I said, taking the suitcase from her and leading her in before she could change her mind.

Once we were inside, just like Mom, she got down to the business of wondering what to make for dinner.

I showed her the few TV dinners still left in the freezer.

"That's not a proper dinner," she said, wrinkling her nose, again just like Mom would do—that is, if Mom ever had frozen dinners in the freezer to begin with. "There's still time to go to the grocery store before it closes."

So that's what we did, her and me, getting the fixings to make her terrific cold chicken salad.

"What smells so good?" Bess asked, entering the kitchen as I helped Eleanor prepare things.

"Are you staying for dinner?" Eleanor asked.

"I could," Bess offered.

"All right," Eleanor said.

I felt so happy then, thinking how the three of us would be having dinner together again, just like we did that one time before, almost like we were a family.

But then I thought of something.

"Can Buster come, too?" I asked.

I don't think I ever told you this, Michael Collins, but I used to dream of being a member of the Girl Scouts of America. Somehow, it never worked out. At school, though, sometimes I would hear girls like Delores Doyle and Lisa Burke talking about things they'd learned in Girl Scouts. And one was a little song called "Make New Friends." Is your daughter, Kate, a Girl Scout? If so, maybe you know it already. If not, it's about keeping old friends, even when you make new ones; about how new friends are like silver, but old friends are like gold.

Now, I know Eleanor and Bess aren't my friends. They're my sisters. And them coming home to be with me, even if Mrs. Whitaker had to talk Bess into it, was a fine thing. But I didn't want to get so lost in the fineness of it all that I forgot Buster.

"Of course," Eleanor said, not looking up from the chopping she was doing. "He's your best friend, isn't he?"

"That's right," I said. "He's my gold."

Then I went to call him.

Dinner with the four of us that night was a festive affair, with everyone talking at once sometimes. There was only one bad moment.

Eleanor had just asked if we'd watched the moonwalk three days ago, which kind of seemed like a stupid question to ask. Hadn't everyone in the world watched that? Of course we had.

"That Neil Armstrong," she said. "He's really something."

"Oh, I guess he's all right," I said. "But you know, Michael Collins is the best one."

"What?" Eleanor said.

Before I could tell her why, or even remind her about how the other day I'd used the example of you to show her there's still time to change her life if she really wants something enough, Bess rolled her eyes.

"Never mind, then," I said, "but he is."

Then Buster suggested we all go look at the kittens, and everything was fine again, because kittens will do that for you.

So that's one terrific thing that happened today, Eleanor coming home. But there's even more. Because today, everyone in the world heard Neil Armstrong talking to us from space, just one day before you all are supposed to land back at home, and here is what he said to us:

We would like to give special thanks to all the Americans who built the spacecraft; who did the construction, design, the tests, and put their hearts and all their abilities into those craft. To those people, tonight, we give a special thank you, and to all the other people that are listening and watching tonight, God bless you. Good night from Apollo 11.

Well, I'll give Neil Armstrong one thing. Thanking everyone like that—it does show manners. Although I do think it's a bit much, him thinking it's okay to speak for all of you.

But never mind that now.

Just one more day, Michael Collins, just one more day.

And then you'll be home.

Or not.

I'm still refusing to think about everything that could still go wrong, so all I'll say to you now is:

God bless you, and good night from Planet Earth.

Sincerely yours,
Mamie

Dear Michael Collins,

Today, eight days, three hours and eighteen minutes after initial liftoff, Apollo 11 reentered our sky.

Okay, I'll get back to that in just a little bit, but there are some other things I need to tell you about first.

I was down in the kitchen eating my breakfast when Eleanor walked in wearing her bathrobe.

"What are you doing eating cake for breakfast?" she said.

"What are you doing not getting ready for work?" I said.

"I thought I'd call in sick today. I could use a day off, to start thinking about my future. And, you know, the astronauts are coming home."

Well, of course I knew that.

"I figured I'd watch it," she said.

"And I figured if I didn't eat the cake, it'd just go to waste," I said.

"That's no kind of breakfast," she said.

I shrugged. Sure, I was happy to have her there. But I'd managed just fine on my own when I had to and I wasn't about to start apologizing for my breakfast choices now.

She stared at me for a bit. But finally she shrugged, too.

Then she got out a knife since I'd already washed the one I'd used and she cut herself a big slice of the leftover Moonwalk Party cake, which was really just a few pieces of the part that had the blue frosting.

"You make this?" she said. "It's good."

"You've got blue lips," I said.

She pointed. "So do you." Then she yelled upstairs, "Bess, wake up and get down here before the cake's all gone and the excitement's all over!"

I didn't think anything short of a shout in the face or a physical jostling ever worked to wake up Bess, but she came down for that.

The three of us finished off the rest of the Moonwalk Party cake, screaming "Blue lips!" at each other every few minutes. Then we got ready for our days, which mostly involved the others getting dressed and me calling up Buster to tell him to come on over.

The night before, when Buster had come for dinner, he hadn't brought any Tang with him because that was not a NASA-related event, but today was, so he did.

A whole pitcher of it.

We each got a big glass of it, and then we lined up seated on the couch—Buster and me in the middle, with Eleanor on my other side and Bess on his—to watch everything on the TV.

These past few days I hadn't let myself dwell too much on any of the bad things that could still happen, but I couldn't stop myself now. What if there wasn't enough resin on your ship? What if you burned up on reentry? What if you were going too fast? What if the parachutes didn't deploy?

So many what-ifs, and not a thing I could do about a single one of them.

We were sitting there waiting, at the edges of our seats, when I heard a car in the driveway, then a second car, a door slam, another door slam. And finally the door in the kitchen opening.

"Hello?" my mom's voice called. "Anybody home?"

"In here!" I called.

And then there she was, followed by my dad.

Neither of them looked any different to me, yet I felt like I must look different. So much had happened while they were gone.

"Oh!" Buster said, seeing them. "I'd better go get some more Tang!"

"No," I said, pulling him back. "I don't want you to miss it."

"We're not too late?" my dad asked.

I shook my head, pointed at the TV. "No. They should be back any time now."

"Campbell had kittens!" Buster announced.

"Oh!" my mom said.

Since the four of us took up the whole couch, my parents sat on the floor. It's not that I wasn't happy they were back, but I needed to watch to make sure you were okay.

And then there you were, in the sky, like I said before: eight days, three hours, and eighteen minutes after your initial liftoff, there you were again.

Only you looked so small. No more Saturn V. No more *Eagle* lunar module—Buster had explained to me how after Armstrong and Aldrin re-docked with you the day after their moonwalk, you'd jettisoned the *Eagle* and now it was back down on the moon, where it will remain forever. Nothing left of Apollo 11 anymore except for the one remaining module, the *Columbia*, looking so small now as it came back toward Earth. You'd needed everything else to get you where you wanted to be in the world. Now the *Columbia* was all that was left to bring you home.

But—oh!—there were those parachutes. And—oh!—there you were, splashing down in the water.

The announcer on TV said you had splashed down several hundred miles from Pearl Harbor. I know about Pearl Harbor from school. It is a place in Hawaii where a terrible thing happened. I guess now, though, it's a place where good things can happen, too. That's funny, isn't it? How even when there's bad, in the very same place there can be good?

As soon as what was left of Apollo 11 made that big splash in the Pacific Ocean, a terrific cheer went up in our living room, so loud it must have rivaled the one at Mission Control in Houston. Bess cheered and Eleanor cheered and my mom cheered and even my dad, who actually said, "That's the most amazing thing I've ever seen!" The only people not cheering were Buster and me.

That's because of something Buster had told me the day before: Even if you survived reentry, even if none of the other million things that could go wrong didn't, no one really knew what the recovery ship would find when they opened the hatch. No matter how many of those million things had gone right, one thing could have still gone wrong and you'd all be dead inside there.

So as the others cheered, again I felt Buster's hand

take mine, and I was so grateful for it, and for the goodness and the friendship and the sheer decency and the *everything* that is him, and then Buster and I just watched, together, as if no one else in the world were there, as the men on the USS *Hornet* opened the hatch.

And, oh, Michael Collins, there you were, there all of you were coming out of the hatch, safe and alive, and finally, Buster and I could cheer, too, which we did, even jumping up and down and hugging while we did it.

Buster says you'll have to go right into quarantine, in case you picked up germs on the moon, and that the quarantine could take a while. But I'm not worried about that part. You've made it this far, and there is just no way that any moon germs can stop you now.

"That Neil Armstrong," my dad said. "No matter what a person thinks about the space race or the government spending so much money on it, he really is an American hero, isn't he?"

I thought about this and how Buster had once explained to me that what was most important to him about Apollo 11 was that, unlike the comic-book heroes that he would always still love, these astronauts were real, live superheroes, and I knew Buster was right. And I thought about what you real, live superheroes had shown me.

Back when this all started—with Mrs. Collins my teacher asking the class what we all wanted to be when we grow up, the boys saying astronauts and the girls wanting to marry astronauts—do you remember me telling you about that, and about how funny I thought it was that the boys all wanted to be the thing and the girls all wanted to marry the thing? And how I wanted to do neither, yet I didn't know what I did want to do?

Well, I still don't know.

But I'll tell you this:

If we can do this, if we can put a man on the moon, then there's more than just the black-and-white, the two paths those kids see. If we can do this, the sky's the limit. No, scratch that, because obviously that's not a limit anymore—you all broke that limit! If we can do this, then anyone can do anything.

I can do anything.

Someday I will figure out what I want to do. And I'll also figure out how to stay and go at the same time. By that I mean it occurred to me that in order to stay with the ship for Armstrong and Aldrin, you had to leave Mrs. Collins your wife and Kate your daughter, and your other children, behind. So I think now there must be ways to go off into the world and have adventures, to do the work that is important to you, while still somehow staying with those who matter most. Perhaps it is in how you conduct yourself and how you hold people in your heart. And home should not hold you back.

I saw my dad cover my mom's hand with his then, just like Buster had covered mine, and I figured that must be what fixed them.

My dad had finally found romance.

Still, that didn't stop me from saying: "Maybe he is, but Michael Collins is the best one."

My dad tore his eyes away from what was happening on the TV and turned to me, a puzzled look on his face.

"Why would you say that, sweet pea?"

"Because he is," I said, and I didn't even care that I knew Bess was rolling her eyes at me again. I'd just say what I needed to say.

"Sure," I said, "it's fine for people to go off and have adventures, it's fine for men to walk on the moon. But they couldn't have done what they did if they hadn't had him to wait for them, if he hadn't stayed with the ship. How would they have come home again? Because, sure, getting there was a fine thing. But that would have been nothing if they hadn't been able to get back. Michael Collins did that, and I'll bet you anything that those one hundred and eighty-four people who graduated ahead of him at the cadet academy are just kicking themselves right now for ever thinking they were better than he is. Because nothing, none of this, would have come out right if it wasn't for him."

"I didn't know you felt so strongly about this," my dad said.

I couldn't believe I'd spoken that way to him. I'd never spoken that way to my dad, or anybody, not in my whole life.

"Well, I do," I said, folding my arms against my chest.

"Huh," my dad said. "I never thought about it like that."

And you know what, Michael Collins? None of them tried to tell me I was wrong about what I'd said, not even Bess.

"You haven't even hugged us hello yet," my mom said then.

Immediately, I saw the error of my ways and I flew into her arms and then my dad's because of course I was glad, so glad, to have them both back. A part of me was still mad at them for leaving me in the first place, but the relief and the glad more than outweighed the mad.

"Did you have fun while we were gone?" my dad said, ruffling my hair.

"What did you do while we were gone?" my mom said. "No one was ever home whenever we tried to call, or else the line was busy."

Of *course* they'd tried to call. How could I have ever doubted it? They loved me. They'd always loved me.

I thought about all the times I'd taken the phone off the hook. I would bet anything that whenever I was out of the house—just my luck—that was when one of them had tried to call. And I also realized that all four of them hadn't so much abandoned me as that each one thought someone else had been looking out for me. My parents thought Eleanor had been here the whole time. Eleanor thought Bess was here. Even Bess had figured I'd just call Eleanor and she'd come home.

Of course, you and I both know that wasn't the case.

But what would be the point in telling them that now?

Maybe someday we'd talk about it, but not today.

I'd been fine.

I am fine.

Then I thought about how everything that happened was a little bit like nesting dolls. Do you know what those are, Michael Collins? Since you have a daughter, Kate, who is just my age, which is still ten, you might. But if not, I will tell you.

Nesting dolls are a set of wooden dolls, with each one being smaller in size, nesting inside one another—just like the name would have you think—from smallest to largest. I thought then how, in our family of nesting dolls, one at a time, they'd all been taken apart and away, even Campbell, until all that was left was me. And how now they'd all come back together again.

Because we were together right then, Michael Collins. In that moment, we were.

I knew it might not last, couldn't, wouldn't.

Eleanor would go away again soon.

Bess would go away to college or for some other reason before too many more years passed.

As for my parents, sure, they were back together now. They even looked happier that way than they had in a very long time. My dad told me later they'd decided that in the fall my mom would go back to school and then maybe get a job she would like, something other than just taking care of our home.

I thought that would make her happier. Certainly, my dad did. But who ever really knew? They'd come apart once. It could always happen again.

For now, though, for this one moment, we were back together again, and all of us, the whole country even, were together in wishing you well, all at the same time. And it was the most amazing thing to feel that, to feel the oneness of it.

But I couldn't explain all that. It was too much to try to say, and besides, no one would ever understand it except for you.

And Buster.

It seemed to me then there was only one thing that really mattered.

"I stayed with the ship," I finally said. "I stayed with the ship."

Sincerely yours,
Mamie

December 14, 1969

Dear Mamie,

I'm sorry it's taken so long to reply, but as I'm sure you've already guessed, I've been a little busy. This is the first free moment I've had in a very long time.

Thank you so much for all your kind letters.

I wanted to be sure you knew how appreciated they have been. And I also wanted to be sure someone told you:

You did a great job.

I know you said you don't want to be an astronaut— or marry one!—but if you ever change your mind, NASA would be lucky to have you, because you are *amazing*.

Really, Mamie, you did a great job.

From My Whole Family to Yours,
Wishing You the Merriest of Christmases,

Michael Collins

Author's Note

I was just seven years old when the astronauts walked on the moon, which, if you do the math, makes me even older now than Mamie's parents are in the book, the parents Mamie thinks of as *really old*. Despite all the years that have passed since then, I can still remember the excitement of staying up late with my brother, Seth, and our parents to watch it happen. I can still remember the excitement of that whole period in history, and I hope I have conveyed that in this book.

The excitement was real, but while I have read a lot about Apollo 11, it's important to keep in mind that this is a work of fiction. This means that in spite of my best efforts, it is entirely possible that I have made some errors. Should you discover any, I hope you will forgive me because, like Buster, I'm not a rocket scientist!

Lauren Baratz-Logsted
Danbury, Connecticut

Acknowledgments

It takes a village to launch a book out into the world from where it begins in an author's head. For this particular book, I would like to thank the following villagers:

Laura Whitaker, for letting me hear the phone line crackle between us when I first shared this idea with you, and for so much more.

Margaret Ferguson, for seeing Michael Collins the way I see Michael Collins; for being an astonishing editor and a charming correspondent; and for saying those four little words every author longs to hear—"I love this book"—and then going it one better by adding, "This book makes me happy."

Farrar Straus Giroux, for publishing this book, thereby making it possible for me to say, "I've had a book published by Farrar Straus Giroux!"

Lauren Catherine, Bob Gulian, Andrea Schicke Hirsch, Greg Logsted, Rob Mayette, and Krissi Petersen Schoonover, for mutual writing support whenever we can on Friday nights.

Greg Logsted, for always believing.

Jackie Logsted, for being even better than the moon.

Finally, thank you to readers everywhere. Like Buster, you are good and decent and *everything*, and I am so grateful.

Suggested Reading

Collins, Michael. *Flying to the Moon: An Astronaut's Story*. New York: Farrar Straus Giroux, 1994.

Floca, Brian. *Moonshot: The Flight of Apollo 11*. New York: Richard Jackson Books, Atheneum, 2009.

Stein, R. Conrad. *The Story of Apollo 11: First Man on the Moon*, 2nd ed. New York: Children's Press, 1992.

Thimmesh, Catherine. *Team Moon: How 400,000 People Landed Apollo 11 on the Moon*. Boston: Houghton Mifflin, 2006.

Wallace, Karen. *Rockets and Spaceships*. New York: DK Readers, 2011.

Wilkinson, Philip. *Spacebusters: The Race to the Moon*. New York: DK Readers, 2012.

I also recommend doing Wikipedia searches for "Michael Collins" and "Apollo 11."